Your wife. Your bride...

When Bo heard Holly come out of the bathroom, he went to her.

She'd just climbed onto the bed when she saw him come through the door. He glimpsed white cotton, modest and sweet, as she pulled the covers over her chest.

But there was that look in her eyes again.

The wanting.

The needing.

I do, she'd said earlier today at the altar. And he'd said it, too.

I do.

He went to her bedside and, as her eyes widened, he slipped a hand behind her head, leaning over.

She hitched in a breath, just before he pressed his lips to her forehead.

"Night, darling," he said, pulling himself away before he destroyed everything.

Dear Reader,

Welcome back to Big Sky Country!

I've had the pleasure of working on some previous Montana Mavericks novels, and every opportunity I get to plunge into these stories, I have the best of times. But this book brought to me my favorite hero of them all—Bo Clifton.

He's a bit of a sweet talker, a gentleman and a scoundrel—how could anyone resist this combination? He meets his match in Holly Pritchett, a woman who's pregnant and down on her luck. At first, she doesn't seem like Bo's type—she's younger, practical-minded, hardly made of the stuff that usually catches a notorious bachelor's eye.

But when she does, the sparks sure fly!

After you read all about Bo and Holly, I'd love for you to join me at www.crystal-green.com for contests, my blog and up-to-the-day news!

All the best,

Crystal Green

WHEN THE COWBOY SAID "I DO"

CRYSTAL GREEN

Silhouette®
SPECIAL EDITION®
Published by Silhouette Books
America's Publisher of Contemporary Romance

Special thanks and acknowledgment to Crystal Green for her contribution to the Montana Mavericks: Thunder Canyon Cowboys continuity.

SILHOUETTE BOOKS

ISBN-13: 978-0-373-65554-0

WHEN THE COWBOY SAID "I DO"

This edition published by arrangement with Harlequin Books S.A.

For questions and comments about the quality of this book please contact us at Customer_eCare@Harlequin.ca.

Visit Silhouette Books at www.eHarlequin.com

Printed in U.S.A.

Books by Crystal Green

Silhouette Special Edition

Beloved Bachelor Dad #1374
**The Pregnant Bride* #1440
**His Arch Enemy's Daughter* #1455
**The Stranger She Married* #1498
**There Goes the Bride* #1522
***Her Montana Millionaire* #1574
**The Black Sheep Heir* #1587
The Millionaire's Secret Baby #1668
†*A Tycoon in Texas* #1670
††*Past Imperfect* #1724
The Last Cowboy #1752
The Playboy Takes a Wife #1838
~*Her Best Man* #1850
§*Mommy and the Millionaire* #1887
§*The Second-Chance Groom* #1906
§*Falling for the Lone Wolf* #1932
‡*The Texas Billionaire's Bride* #1981

*Kane's Crossing
**Montana Mavericks: The Kingsleys
†The Fortunes of Texas: Reunion
††Most Likely To…
~Montana Mavericks: Striking it Rich
§The Suds Club
‡The Foleys and the McCords

Silhouette Romance

Her Gypsy Prince #1789

Silhouette Bombshell

The Huntress #28
Baited #112

Harlequin Blaze

Playmates #121
Born to Be Bad #179
Innuendo #261
Jinxed! #303
"Tall, Dark & Temporary"
The Ultimate Bite #334
One for the Road #387
Good to the Last Bite #426
When the Sun Goes Down #472

CRYSTAL GREEN

lives near Las Vegas, where she writes for Silhouette Special Edition and Harlequin Blaze. She loves to read, overanalyze movies and TV programs, practice yoga and travel when she can. You can read more about her at www.crystal-green.com, where she has a blog and contests. Also, you can follow her on Facebook at www.facebook.com/people/Chris-Marie-Green/1051327765 and Twitter at www.twitter.com/ChrisMarieGreen.

To the rest of the Montana Mavericks authors—
you guys have the right stuff.

Chapter One

"I'm really in it deep, Erika, and I have no idea what to do."

Holly Pritchett sat in a booth at DJ's Rib Shack, subtly cradling an arm over her tiny swell of a belly. She wore yet another massive sweater, the better to hide the little secret she'd been keeping for the past seven months.

"What couldn't you tell me on the phone?" Erika Rodriguez asked while tossing her purse into the booth and taking a seat, all while fixing a sympathetic brown gaze on her friend. She'd come straight to the restaurant from her office here, at the Thunder Canyon Resort, so her dark hair was pulled back and she was dressed in a conservative skirt suit. She looked just like the put-together big sister figure Holly needed right now.

Around them, the dinner crowd murmured from the

long family-style tables in the main area. Sepia-tinged pictures of cowboys and ranches hung on the walls, along with a painted mural showcasing the town's history. The heavy sweet/tangy aroma of the restaurant's original barbecue sauce permeated the air, but that wasn't exactly what was tightening Holly's stomach.

She took a deep breath and stopped touching her belly, just in case anyone might be looking. Her baby—Hopper, she liked to call him or her because of the tiny jumps Holly would feel every so often—didn't need anyone knowing what straits good old Mommy was in.

"It's my father," Holly said, anxiety chasing her even now, although she tried to quell it for the baby's sake. "I think he knows."

Erika closed her eyes, clearly guessing where this was going. "How could he tell? You've been hiding it really well under those clothes."

"I know. I've been carrying small and haven't popped yet." But as she'd always been on the skinny side and she'd liked to wear snugger clothing, it had to have been the big skirts and sweaters that had made her dad suspicious. "You should've heard him before I left the ranch. 'Seems you've been eating better than usual since you graduated, Hol.' And he had this expression on his face, like he meant something else entirely. I must've had some kind of telling look on my face, too, because then he said, 'You didn't just put on a few pounds, did you?'"

Erika frowned just as the waitress arrived at an adjacent table, seating another customer.

Holly had enough presence of mind to glance over before she dared to continue. But the new diner's back was to them as he set up a laptop computer. A Stetson rode low over his face, further obscuring any features.

When he took off his sheepskin jacket and put it on the bench, Holly couldn't help but notice his broad back.

She saw him putting in some earbuds that were connected to his computer as the waitress left. Holly went on, feeling secure that he wouldn't be able to hear them.

"Then Dad asked me straight out if I was pregnant."

Erika hadn't spared much more than a glance at the new arrival, either. "And you told him all about Alan."

Holly pursed her lips.

"You *didn't* tell him about Alan dumping you so he could accept that law clerk position overseas?"

"I know I should have, but I heard myself saying something entirely different instead."

Erika's big-sis eyebrow shot up.

Not good. The two of them had struck up a friendship during the days when Holly's father had been buying up more land for the family ranch, and he'd brought her to the real estate office where Erika had been working as a receptionist. While Holly had waited in the lounge, she and Erika had gotten to talking, finding that the two of them had a lot in common. From that point on, Holly had looked forward to each visit as their camaraderie had grown.

Basically, a raised eyebrow from Holly's surrogate big sis was just as bad as any disappointment Holly's father could wield.

She scrambled to explain herself. "It was the look

on Dad's face… And when he said, 'I thought I raised you to be smarter than this'… Well, I just heard myself saying something to him that I never dreamed would come out of my mouth."

It had been a comment that goody-two-shoes, straightforward Holly would've never dared.

"And…?" Erika asked.

She exhaled, then said, "I told my dad that he shouldn't fret about me and the baby because I've got a fiancé, and he'll be coming into town in a few weeks after he finishes up a job."

Erika didn't react for a moment. She only stared at Holly.

Of course, that meant Holly needed to explain herself even more.

"Then I said to him that I'd been keeping quiet about everything because I wanted to make the engagement and baby announcement with my fiancé, together, after he arrived."

It looked as if Erika wanted to say a million finger-wagging things, but she limited herself. "So what are you going to do if Alan *doesn't* come back to you? How are you going to explain *that* to your family? Because I know your brothers. The three of them will hunt that guy down and drag him back to the States by his hair."

"I didn't exactly mention Alan's name." Holly traced the edge of the menu in front of her. "I've already accepted that he's not going to come back. But I had to tell Dad something. You know how he is."

"Yes—Daddy Pritchett thinks the world of his golden girl. But, Holly, why didn't you just tell him the truth about Alan? It's going to break your father's heart even more when he finds out you lied to him."

Holly was feeling sicker by the moment.

Erika continued. "And I know how *you* are, too. You're just as disappointed in yourself, and it's tearing you apart to have this dilemma."

Their waitress strolled up to take their orders, and for a minute or two, Holly was able to put on one of those "everything's okay" faces that she was so good at.

Another lie.

Good heavens, before now, Holly hadn't told very many of them, and they sure did weigh.

After the waitress picked up the menus, both Holly and Erika sipped their water, the moment just as awkward and disappointment-laden as Holly had feared. Her gaze wandered to the nearby table, where the lone occupant sat, still facing away from them.

He was dressed in shined-up boots and new blue jeans. Thick blond hair ruffled from taking off his cowboy hat, which he'd set next to him on the bench by his coat. His computer open on the table as he used those earbuds to listen to whatever news report he was clearly monitoring onscreen.

In spite of herself, Holly lingered on his wide back, the muscles outlined clearly under his Western shirt. Her skin tingled, just as if someone had brought summer to October and the sun was heating her body....

Then, realizing what she was doing, she looked away.

Worst time ever to be looking at some cowboy.

Erika had taken another glance at him, too, before returning her attention to Holly, then placing her water on the table.

"No matter what went on with your dad, I'm glad

you called. We're going to find a way to get you out of this."

Holly smiled, relief coming out in the gesture. "I knew I could count on you." Erika had gone through her own period of single-motherhood before her fiancé, Dillon Traub, had come along. Her two-year old daughter, Emilia, adored him. Life was good for their new family.

And it could be the same for Holly if she could just dig herself out of this.

Still, she sighed. "Who would've thought a girl like me would end up in this situation? I had so many different plans..."

"Sometimes our passions get the better of us." Erika smiled sadly, obviously remembering how her boyfriend had ditched her once upon a time, too. "Even a law student like you can find yourself veering from your path."

"I was an *almost* law student," Holly said, a tinge of longing in her voice. "Never quite got to grad school."

But then she discreetly rested her arm over her baby bump, and smiled. The moment she'd found out she was pregnant, she'd promised herself no regrets. Not even for meeting Alan.

"Knowing the determined Holly Pritchett," Erika said, "I don't doubt that you'll come out of even a moment like this shining."

"It'll take some work." She laughed slightly. "It's hard to believe that I ever thought I'd get through all my schooling, then return to my hometown a complete success. A lawyer who champions the downtrodden, right? Then, I met *him*."

"Alan the rat."

"Yes—a huge, scurrying rat. I never in a thousand years thought that he wasn't just as crazy about me as I was about him. I was too busy picturing ways for me to march into Thunder Canyon as the best wife and mother in creation to notice that he wasn't as excited as I was."

"I know exactly how you feel. But I know this, too—you're better off without him."

Spoken by someone who'd lived it and learned it.

"You're right," Holly said. "I guess I thought I could talk him into being a family man. I truly believed there was even a way to keep *my* family from knowing that the pregnancy wasn't planned. I was still going to come off as Miss In-Control."

It'd been absolutely inconceivable to Holly that her plans wouldn't come to fruition.

Then Alan's job offer had changed everything.

Holly could still hear him the night he'd come home to their apartment near campus with the news of his clerking offer in a high-powered London firm.

I've been thinking, Hol... This is an amazing opportunity for me... I'll pay for our child's upbringing, don't you worry about it, but I can't commit any more than that right now...

Then, the final blow after she'd told him to get out.

I never told you I wanted children with you. It just happened. I got trapped...

The last thing Holly wanted was a husband who felt like that rat in a cage, so she'd let him gnaw his way out of it.

Erika reached across the table to hold her friend's hand. "You'll still stand proud and strong, just like any Pritchett."

Holly's shoulders slumped a little at that. "Yeah—standing on a lie that just whizzed right out of my mouth before I could stop it."

"Holly..." Erika looked as if she was going to ask something hard. She didn't disappoint. "If Alan somehow experienced a change of heart and decided to send for you, what would you do?"

The question clawed into Holly. It had already found a painful place in her these past months, while she'd lived at her father's house, working at a temporary, homebound, online data input job to save money, not only to pay off her college loans, but because she'd told Alan to keep his paychecks to himself and go to hell in the meantime.

She hugged her arms over her belly, not caring now if anyone saw.

A child needed a father.

So if Alan ever wanted to come back, would she say yes?

God, she just didn't know. It wasn't that *she* wanted him in her life again. It was about what her baby needed.

Holly just didn't have any answers, and that went double when it came to realizing who *she* even was these days: the girl who'd grown up under such high expectations from everyone? The one who'd planned her life out to a T?

Or this flailing single mom?

"I have no idea what I'd do, Erika," Holly said softly. "It'd be nice to have the support. Dad can't give it to me because he's got his hands full enough with the ranch. My brothers can't spare anything, either. I wouldn't even dare ask. But Alan doesn't even call me to check on how the baby's doing. Why would I want someone like that involved with us?"

The waitress arrived with their salads, so Holly and Erika paused. Then their server went to the cowboy at the next table, who took out his earbuds and glanced up at her, revealing his profile.

And a smile to beat all smiles.

Just seeing it almost knocked Holly out of the booth.

That blond hair...That profile, with its cut jaw, firm chin, full lips and straight nose...

She narrowed her gaze at him. He looked familiar.

Her heart scampered around in her chest, as if chasing around his identity.

When the waitress left, she was wearing a won-over grin.

The cowboy put his earbuds back in, turning back to his computer.

"I swear," Erika said, a note of amusement in her voice.

"What?"

"Bo Clifton. He's got enough charm to talk the wings off of a butterfly."

Now Holly's pulse jerked.

Bo Clifton?

Erika had her big sis eyebrow going again. "I know you were visiting your cousin during the summer when his mayoral campaign got started, but didn't you recognize him the second he walked in?"

"Sure." Duh. Beauregard Clifton's image was only plastered all over Thunder Canyon, smiling out from those Golden Days Ahead with Bo! posters.

But Holly was also recalling another Bo Clifton....

She faced Erika again, acting as if she hadn't been gaping at him. "It's just that I haven't seen him in ages."

"He's back in town in a big way now. He moved out of Thunder Canyon years ago to buy a second spread near Bozeman."

"Besides the one his parents left him here before they moved?"

"Yes."

"Bozeman." Holly entertained a flash of fantasy: what would've happened if she had run into Bo in the city near her college? If she had remembered him and he had remembered her as he gave her one of those hot smiles she'd seen the waitress enjoying…?

She shook it off. "So he wants to be mayor of Thunder Canyon. That's quite a job."

Governing a town that had grown by leaps and bounds after a gold rush, then the exploding popularity of the Thunder Canyon Resort. But the economy had started sinking during the last couple of years, and it had hit this small town especially hard.

"Bo's up to it," Erika said. "He saw what was going on here and decided he could do something about it."

"All I have to say is that I'm glad someone besides Arthur Swinton threw his hat into the ring." Holly shook her head. "Him and his old way of thinking are enough to drive this town deeper into the ground."

"A lot of the younger crowd would agree with you. Sounds like Bo's got your vote, too."

"We'll see." Holly picked at her salad, trying to control her heartbeat, which was still bopping around. "Way back when, our families would have the occasional barbecue, and he was even pressed into babysitting me and my brothers a few times, too."

Bo was thirteen years older, a sun-kissed teenage cowboy who liked to buck the system—or so she'd heard in town every so often. And she'd crushed on him hard until other more accessible boys had come along.

She remembered Bo, all right.

The waitress stopped by to refill their water glasses. "Anything else for you gals before your ribs get here?"

Holly and Erika said no, and as their server disappeared, they started to talk again.

Until they realized that someone had gotten out of his seat and was standing near their table.

Holly jumped at the sight of Bo Clifton.

She couldn't catch a breath, what with him and his broad shoulders and charming smiles. His skin was tanned, and it made his forget-me-not blue eyes stand out like memories that had never quite left her.

"Ladies," he said.

"Bo." Erika nodded cordially. She'd worked with him recently on a rally at the Frontier Days festival, so she was obviously comfortable with him moseying on over here. "Do you remember Holly Pritchett?"

"Indeed I do."

He extended his hand to Holly, who stared at it a moment, as if debating whether or not it'd be a good idea to touch him.

Temptation. A large hand like Bo's enveloping her in warm skin.

Pregnancy hormones flitted around in her like little red sparks.

And that's all it was, too—her body. A bunch of hormones that constantly wanted to get into mischief.

It had nothing to do with this cowboy in particular.

When Holly shook his hand, it was warm all right. Roughened, just like the skin of a man who was used to a good day of work.

When Holly let go of him—maybe too soon, because Erika was watching her with curiosity—she tucked her hand under her leg, trying to get rid of the delicious shivers that were tingling from her fingers and up the length of her arm.

"Good to see you," she said to Bo.

Now please go.

But he was doing no such thing.

In fact, he rested his hands on the table and leaned over to meet her gaze. And what he said next shocked her with its straight-to-the-point boldness.

"I couldn't help but hear a few scraps of your conversation. And if you don't mind me saying so, Holly, Erika is right—you're going to find a way out of your situation. In fact, I've got all the troubleshooting you're ever going to need right here."

Bo Clifton was a man who didn't believe in small talk unless it was absolutely necessary, but apparently Holly Pritchett could've used a better lead-in.

Both she and Erika Rodriguez merely sat and stared at him as if he was the world's biggest party crasher.

But a man who was going to turn this town back around needed the gumption to tackle matters headfirst. Just look where pretty talk and politics had gotten Thunder Canyon—into a fine mess, a recession that rivaled even the most downtrodden towns in the great U.S. of

A. The type of change Bo was going to bring would take some big-time blunt talking, and he'd been good at mixing that with persuasive words all of his life.

Yup, running things in Thunder Canyon was the job for him, and as he'd sat there listening to Holly Pritchett's woes, it'd occurred to Bo that he had a way to solve both his challenges and hers.

As he smiled down at her, his belly warmed with appreciation. She'd gone from an all-knees-and-elbows girl whom he'd babysat every once in a blue moon to this—a cherry-cheeked, blond-curled, blue-eyed woman. She was like a fresh breeze blowing through Thunder Canyon.

But she was clearly in trouble, too.

Not that he'd intended to overhear Holly and Erika while he'd sat at his table, grabbing a quick bite after doing some business with his cousin, Grant, up here at the resort. After the waitress had seated Bo and well before he'd even turned on the volume of his computer to catch the nightly news, he'd heard the women talking, so he'd kept the volume off, telling himself that he would crank it up soon enough.

But that had never happened, because with each new revelation from Holly, a plan had formed in Bo's mind. It was pretty radical—maybe even drastic. But, then again, when had Bo ever been traditional?

Ever optimistic about his opportunities to bring about solutions, Bo pressed his advantage now.

"It seems," he added, "that you need a husband as much as I need a wife."

Bo hadn't thought the ladies' mouths could've opened any wider in stunned disbelief, but they managed it.

"Now, just hear me out," he said, keeping his tone

reasonable. "I'm not talking nonsense. I have a mutually beneficial offer that you'll at least want to consider."

"Whoa," Erika said as Bo grinned and slid into the booth next to her so he could face Holly.

But *she* was still watching him as if he'd popped up out of the dirt like a prairie dog with its hair on fire.

Holly finally spoke. "You can't be serious."

"I am."

He understood her surprise, but Bo wasn't much bothered by his plan. Long ago, his parents had made a mockery out of marriage. A fake one would surely go smoother than the so-called real thing.

She sure looked like a breezy young woman fresh out of college, but she had a commanding tone when she wanted to use it. "You sat there with your earplugs in, pretending to be busy, but all the while you were listening to our private conversation—things I haven't even shared with my family?"

"I apologize for the circumstances, but believe me when I say my intentions are on the up and up."

She went back to staring at him. Now he felt like a Martian.

Understandable. "Pardon my saying so, but years ago, our parents saw me fit enough to look after you, Holly. And good neighbors don't stop being good neighbors just because some years have passed."

Holly shot a where-did-this-alien-come-from? glance to Erika.

"Here's the thing," he said, leaning on the table. "There's nothing I want more than to help Thunder Canyon, and I'd venture a guess that this would be near the top of your own list, since your family is still living here. And I know just how important family is to you. This town has been a real home for both of us."

"Arthur Swinton would argue that you can't really claim Thunder Canyon as home since you chose to live near Bozeman instead of your ranch here."

"He'd be wrong. I'm back in town every summer. More importantly, Thunder Canyon was where my family put down roots. Their blood is here, too."

Holly seemed to realize what he was talking about—the long-ago murder of his uncle, who'd been killed alongside the father of his cousin by marriage, Stephanie Clifton.

And Bo never wanted Thunder Canyon to go back to those days. He'd be *damned* if the town ever sunk so low again.

He hadn't meant to play that card, so he tucked it back in where no one could see it, just as he always did. Helplessness got a man nowhere.

"Just hear me out for five minutes," he said.

When he got the feeling that Holly was about to turn him down flat for good, he forged ahead.

"Here are the reasons you need an immediate solution. One—you should avoid stress in your pregnancy, and your strife with your dad is bad for your baby."

Holly blinked, and Bo could tell that she'd thought this over quite carefully even before he'd brought it up.

Score one for the rancher.

"Two," he added, "I can provide the baby with a name and you with a sizable income—much more than you've been getting at that temp job of yours."

"You know that I—?"

"I've had my ears open in Thunder Canyon, as well as here in the Rib Shack."

She still wasn't telling him to go away.

"Three—Arthur Swinton is starting to sling some mud in this campaign. Now, I have a handle on the younger vote in this town. They like what I'm saying about changing some of the things that haven't worked for us. But then there's the old guard who keeps voting Swinton into the town council year after year, even though he's a big part of the reason we've had economic policies that practically set us up for such a fall. Instead of addressing his failures, he's been concentrating on the topic of family values, and he's throwing out some hints about how I'm too young and rebellious to be mayor. I've also heard from his camp that I'm some kind of wild bachelor, an outsider who's going to ruin Thunder Canyon with my unstable, inexperienced ways."

"Don't wild, rebellious guys usually interrupt dinners to make preposterous offers like yours?" Holly asked.

Bo took her feistiness as a good sign and his smile only grew. "It's true that I've done my share of partying in the past, but that doesn't make me less fit to do what needs to be done in Thunder Canyon. And believe me, I'm all for family values—it's just that I've been pretty busy running my businesses to get hitched, and that shouldn't be a mark against me."

"You do like to do things in your own way."

"Yes, I do," he said. "And I like to treat women with all the affection and dignity they deserve. I haven't needed to get married to accomplish that, either."

Holly pulled at the collar of her blue sweater as the pink on her cheeks seemed to intensify.

Her skin… Was it his imagination, or was she glowing ever so slightly?

Then again, she was pregnant. Probably the glow had nothing to do with his suggestive remark.

Either way, he brought himself out of wondering about things of such a nature. Business. This was only about business. The proposal had nothing to do with glowy skin, no matter how smooth it looked. No matter how much he was thinking about what it would feel like if he touched it.

He smiled again. "What I'm trying to say is this—you could really use some good care, whether it involves saving you from an awkward situation with your family, giving you and your baby all you need financially or…"

"Or what?" Holly asked softly.

A heartbeat plugged by, and he found that he didn't have an answer.

But then Holly glanced at the table, as if angry at herself for even asking. Hell, *he* wasn't too happy, either, because he hadn't even been able to finish his damned sentence.

Business.

He just wanted to tell her it would be all business.

Next to him, Erika laughed a little, but Bo knew he had a strong case if he would only hang in there. Untraditional, yes, but perfectly reasonable.

Help me help you, he thought. Just like a good neighbor should.

He played his last hand. "You volunteer for the ROOTS mentor program for teens with Haley Anderson, don't you? And you were planning to be a civic-minded lawyer."

"Yes…"

"Then you're practically made to be a mayor's wife—respectable, community-oriented—if only for long enough to get us both what we want."

Holly's gaze seemed to go a little hazy as she looked into his eyes. Was she thinking of how easy it'd be to go back to her father and tell him that she hadn't been lying about a fiancé after all?

He could only hope.

"Six months," he said. "That's all the commitment I'd be asking for. Long enough for me to win that election and get a foothold in changing things for the better. During that time, you'd also have so many opportunities to pull Thunder Canyon out of its hole, Holly. Come springtime, we can get a quiet annulment and I'll compensate you for your efforts with enough money to make your child's future the best it can be."

His pulse thudded as she continued staring at the table, as if she was running all the scenarios through her mind. He even thought he saw her touch her belly, which seemed pretty small for seven months along.

A few seconds ticked by. Had he done it?

Would she…?

But then she reached for her purse and coat, fumbling out her wallet, then putting money on the table next to her barely touched salad. She made her way out of the booth, gracefully for a pregnant woman. Nonetheless, he got up to help her, but she refused him as Erika put her own money on the table.

"We can get the rest of the food to go," Holly said to her friend, ignoring Bo altogether.

And that's when he saw it all spin by—the opportunity to really do good…his uncle laughing in old photos...his cousins Grant and Elise trying to hold back tears at the funeral so long ago...Bo staring at the coffin, numb until he began comforting himself with dreams about how to change a world that had flown off its axis...

All of it, slipping away.

"Holly," he said. "No matter how crazy my offer might sound, my intentions truly are for the best. Remember that."

She must've heard something in his voice, because when she looked at him again, there was a sort of understanding in her blue gaze.

But it barely had time to seep into him before she said, "Good night, Bo."

Then she walked away, taking Erika with her and leaving behind Bo's hopes for his own future, as well as that of this town he loved.

But if there was one thing Bo wasn't, it was done. Not when he'd seen her looking so thoughtful about what he'd said.

Not when he knew there still might be a chance.

Chapter Two

After getting the rest of their meals boxed up, Holly said good-bye to Erika at the enclosed entrance to the Rib Shack. Her friend needed to run by her resort office and grab some files she'd forgotten to take home with her.

"At least this is going to be a night to remember," Erika said as they shrugged into their coats.

A night to remember, when Bo Clifton had come out of nowhere to propose.

That's when Holly started laughing—incredulous, *Outer Limits* laughter that made Erika join in until they were both wiping tears from their eyes.

Just imagine, Holly thought. *A quickie marriage. Me. Miss Used-to-be-Prim-and-Proper.*

Her laughter faded as the idea slid away.

Married to Bo Clifton…

"It's almost like I dreamed it up." Holly sighed and buttoned her bulky wool coat. "Bo Clifton, to the rescue."

His name. Just saying it felt intriguing. Almost as if conjuring up his smile and the glint in his blue eyes was nice. With most guys, Holly would've run as fast as she could away from him and such a left-field offer, but she'd known Bo and had trusted him years ago.

She'd kind of liked him, too.

More than liked him, way back when.

But that had been ages past, when she'd still worn glittery nail polish. Now they'd both grown up—her into an unsure, expecting mom and him into…

She couldn't quite find the correct description for Bo.

Head case? Delusional fast talker?

All she knew was that she was still tingling a little, just thinking about him.

Holly tossed a scarf around her neck as Erika repeated, "Yeah, Bo to the rescue."

When she paused, Holly thought it might be because two women had come into the Shack's entrance, and Erika wanted to be discreet until the ladies entered the restaurant proper. But there was a kink to Erika's brow, a thoughtful angle.

The cool October night air that had come in through the doorway brushed Holly's cheeks as the couple left her standing with Erika in the entrance.

Her friend finally spoke. "Even though Bo came off oddly, I do think he was being genuine. I can't explain why. Maybe because when I worked with him, I really got a feel for what sort of person he is—and it's a sincere one."

Holly had formed that idea, too. You could tell when someone was running a line of bull—she'd just seen it in Alan too late, and that's why she'd let him go, because she knew he was never going to change.

But Bo?

He hadn't been messing around. There were even a few moments, when she hadn't been thinking he was a loon, that he'd actually made a lot of sense.

A bright future for her child… A chance to make her family still respect her, if she could keep her mistakes with Alan from them…

And there was something else niggling at her that Bo hadn't even addressed. Her dad was as old-fashioned as they came, so how would he look at her baby if he or she was born out-of-wedlock?

A fiancé would legitimize her child.

A fiancé—a well-off rancher and mayoral candidate to boot—would solve so many things.

Erika laid a hand on Holly's arm, as if she was pulling Holly back from a train of thought that was careening off the rails.

"Even if Bo's offer was genuine," she said, "it was really out there. Just think about it—marrying for money and to get you out of a tight spot, not because of love."

"In some other cultures, marriage is considered a business arrangement." The words were out of Holly's mouth before she'd even weighed them.

Erika tilted her head, gauging, so Holly smiled as if she were kidding.

Wasn't she?

Her friend smiled back. "No matter the case, I won't be spreading around what he proposed. Bo's going to be good for this town, and I won't give his opponent any ammunition."

"Sounds like you don't mind having a mercenary-minded guy for mayor."

"If I thought Bo was more dangerous than Arthur Swinton, I would've headed a committee to run him out of town way before this."

They walked into the crisp night, where a cloud cover puffed over the moon. Holly gave her friend a big hug, then said good-night as they parted and Holly headed toward her vehicle, a blue pickup that looked way more at home on her family's ranch than here at the resort, where the few tourists who still visited had parked their jaunty cars and sleek sedans. Luckily, there were the more weather-beaten, practical local trucks and SUVs to balance things out.

Holly's boot steps echoed on the pavement, her long, flowy flannel skirt brushing against her legs as she wrapped her arms around herself.

Without Erika here to act as a Greek chorus, Bo's provocative suggestions nudged her again. And the more Holly thought about them, the more every one of them made sense.

She slowed her pace. Holly Pritchett—straight A student, full-ride scholarship earner, community volunteer. That's all she'd been a year ago, when she'd met Alan.

But how would the woman she was now handle things going forward?

As she searched for her keys in her coat pocket with the hand that wasn't holding her box of takeout, a slight kick came from inside her tummy.

She stopped, touching it.

Did her baby have some kind of opinion about Bo's offer?

Was he or she trying to tell Holly that it would be grand to live a life with all the comforts a child would need? Enough money for college? A mother who wasn't trying to make it on the shoestring budget of a temp job?

Did he or she want a daddy to lend them a name?

The baby gave Holly another swift, soft kick, and her throat went tight.

Six months. That's what Bo had said. Six short months and then she would have so much for her baby.

Except for a real father.

Holly dropped her hand from her stomach, beginning to walk again, but a sound from behind halted her.

A man, softly clearing his throat.

Before Holly even turned around, she knew it was Bo. She could feel his presence on her skin, in the middle of her chest. In the crash of her heartbeats.

Slowly, she looked back at him, finding him under the moonlight, his hat shading most of his face except for that strong chin. A sheepskin coat covered a set of shoulders that could easily carry some of her own burdens.

Pride—or maybe it was just a good dose of common sense—brought Holly to reality.

"You just don't give up, do you?" she asked.

He hitched the strap of his laptop case farther up his shoulder and took a step forward, self-assured, not at all put off by her annoyed tone.

"I'm just seeing that you make it to your car safely," he said.

"Thank you, but there's no need."

She started to walk again, and it seemed that all it took for him to catch up to her was a couple of long steps. It was enough for her to take in the tempting scent of him: shower smells, that sheepskin coat, a hint of warm skin.

Holly's heart flipped, but, even more worrisome, something just below her belly did, too, right in a place that had gotten her into trouble with Alan.

"I didn't mean to scare you off," he said. "It's only that I'm the type who doesn't wait around, turning an idea over in his head all night. When I see a situation that needs righting, I do my best to address it."

"I don't need any righting, Bo."

This particular lie felt just as bad as the bull she'd shoveled out to her dad earlier tonight.

My fiancé's coming into town in a few weeks...

Holly hadn't realized it, but she had slowed down again. She might even have said that she and Bo were strolling at a courting pace, in no hurry to get away from each other.

But by the time that thought hit her, they were at her pickup, and she readied her keys.

"In spite of turning down your offer, I do wish you luck on your campaign," she said. "No one who's been paying attention to Thunder Canyon wants Swinton in charge."

"At least I have your vote instead of your hand."

He grinned, and Holly just about leaned back against her car, her legs losing rigidity.

Bo Clifton.

Damn, he had a presence. Even the way he just stood there, one hand casually propped low on his hip, his body speaking its own laconic language without the benefit of smooth words, made Holly want to melt.

"I suspect," she finally said, "that if you're as good at carrying out some change as you are at talking about it, you'll be fine without help."

He raised a hand and tipped back his hat, allowing the moonlight to fall over more of his face—the perpetual smile lines around his eyes and mouth, that slightly amused glint in his gaze.

"Coming from a woman who does a lot of doing herself," he said, "that means something. People noticed when you came back to town, you know. And you've just started volunteering for ROOTS—they think well of that, too. They talked about how you were going to be a big lawyer someday. They're real proud of you, Holly."

She kept her tongue. How proud were they going to be when her lies hit her smack dab in the face?

"I don't know if you recall it," he said, his voice going lower, as if sensing that soothing was just what she needed right now, "but even back when I was babysitting for you, I could tell you were a force to be reckoned with. You'd never let your older brothers get the better of you. I even had to intercede a time or two when you insisted on roughhousing with them."

"I remember." There'd been one time when Hollis, Nick and Dean had thought it might be fun to box their five-year-old little sister up in a "cardboard house" with duct tape and the works. She'd punched a hole in a wall, raging at her brothers, just as Bo had come to her aid, ripping the box apart and giving her brothers a talking-to for crossing a line.

Now, the child worship of him came rushing back. Holly's hero.

Thunder Canyon's hero, too, if they ended up electing him.

Bo peered off in the distance, out of the parking lot, toward the mountains. Holly watched him for a moment, holding onto the look of him.

A dreamer and doer. Charmed and charming.

She laughed, her nerves still rolling. Standing here in a parking lot with Bo Clifton, childhood crush and, now, candidate for mayor. The man who'd just proposed to her, a near neighbor who was still a stranger.

He laughed a little, too, as if appreciating the absurdity of all this.

"Well, good luck, Bo," she said, holding up her hands, her keys jangling from her fingers.

"You have to admit that I'm not shy about problem solving."

"No, you're not." Holly blew out a breath. "I can't begin to point out all the issues your problem solving would have brought up, though."

"Nothing we couldn't manage."

"Oh, Bo. For starters, after a six-month marriage to you, my child still wouldn't have a father."

"I said I'd provide for him or her for the rest of your lives."

"That's not the same thing."

"No, it's not." He'd sobered at that, but she could still tell he thought his offer had been a damned good one.

"Besides, if Alan ever did come back to Montana, he'd know what was what."

"Not necessarily. What if you and I had started seeing each other while you were at college, right after Alan left you? And what if we'd kept it a secret because you didn't want anyone to think that you were the type who goes from one man to another? It'd be just like you to worry about appearances like that. Maybe your friends didn't even know about us…."

"I told Alan I was pregnant, so how would that explain the baby being yours?"

"Maybe you got a false reading on a home pregnancy test and you were mistaken about the news when you told him. You didn't get pregnant until after he left town, and your baby will just be born early."

Good heavens, this man could spin a tale—and woo her with the very thought of this fictional romance at the same time.

Seduced by Bo…

Holly got ahold of herself. They wouldn't need a story like this, because, first, Alan had made up his mind to leave her and her child, and Holly knew his ambition for what it was—all-consuming. He wouldn't be back.

Second, she wasn't going to say yes to this harebrained scheme.

She presented another reason his plan would never work. "Then there's the whole problem of Swinton. You're much older than I am. He'd jump all over that, saying you're a cradle robber."

Bo rolled his eyes. "I doubt many others would point it out. What are we—about fifteen years apart? Big deal."

"Thirteen," she said, too quickly. She'd added up the difference a long time ago, during the babysitting, journal-writing days when she would scribble down who she wanted to marry someday. But she'd eventually recorded names like Leonardo DiCaprio on those pages, too, so it wasn't as if she'd held herself to the promises of her youth or anything.

Just when she thought Bo might ask her how she could be so precise about their age difference, she said, "But here's the biggest believability issue—no one is going to buy into a marriage between you—the mayoral candidate—and me—the pregnant recent college graduate. They'd think you haunted the Bozeman campus or trolled the bars around the area, and that's just going to justify everything Arthur Swinton says."

He laughed at her honesty.

"I'm not saying I wouldn't have been flattered, though," she added, trying to soften the blow.

"You didn't offend, Holly. It's just that, with everything you say, you prove my point all the more."

"What point?"

"That you were made for what I proposed."

Talk about single-minded. "Bo, I was going to be a lawyer. I can expose the weaknesses in any case or scenario."

"Like the story you told your dad about that fiancé who's coming to town?"

And...*boom*. They were done.

Holly turned to her pickup, unlocking it. She opened the door, ready to pull herself in.

"Uh-uh," Bo said, coming to her side, placing one hand on the small of her back and one on her hip, helping her into her seat, whether or not she wanted it. "I don't care how independent you are."

Once she was behind the wheel, his touch lingered on her, and even through her coat, sweater and skirt, she could feel the outline of his hands—hot, as if the burn would never go away.

The oxygen seemed to dissipate in her lungs, leaving her breathless as he slowly removed himself, backing away. His gaze searched hers, as if he was finding something there that even she wasn't fully aware of.

Or maybe she was.

A father for her baby—even a temporary one...

He grinned, just as if he'd read her mind. She shut the pickup door, the metal rattling.

As she started the truck, he tipped his hat to her in a farewell gesture, still wearing that maddening smile.

It wasn't too far of a drive to the fringes of Thunder Canyon, where the Pritchett spread waited. But as Holly pulled into the graveled drive in front of the ranch house—a log cabin from the 1940s—she wished she'd had a few hundred miles more before she arrived.

She could see the window of the parlor—where she'd had her discussion with her dad before leaving the house to meet with Erika—burning with light. It devoured the beige curtains.

Stilling her nerves, Holly got out of the pickup and went into the cabin, hanging up her coat on a rack nailed to the barn wood wall and kicking some work boots out of the way of the dirt-crusted doormat.

Nice. She was always getting after her brothers when they cut through this entrance rather than the mudroom. They still worked the spread with her father, even though they lived in their own cabins nearby and only spent time in the house when visiting with Dad.

After she removed her own relatively pristine boots and carried them through the foyer, her mood got even darker as she waded through tools and wood from a nightstand someone had decided to repair and abandoned, then a bunch of fishing gear propped against the stairs.

Men.

She was trying to move aside a pole when she heard her dad's soft bark from the parlor.

"Hol?"

Frowning, she backed away from the stairs. "Here, Dad."

She found him sitting on a threadbare settee in front of a crackling fire in the stone hearth. He and his gruff, gray wire-haired miner appearance fit right in among the faded, old-Western velvet upholstery and mahogany furniture her mom had favored. He hadn't changed a thing since she'd died seven years ago of a heart attack—not even the black-and-white photos of places like Tombstone that she'd taken during their quirky ghost town-itinerary honeymoon. Nor the colorful afghan she'd knitted just for him.

The blanket was spread over his legs, but Holly knew he was under it more to be in contact with what his wife had touched rather than to ward off any chill.

Heck, it was almost as if both of her parents were in the room, looking at her with crestfallen expressions.

As Holly's heart sank, too, Bo's voice came to her.

It seems that you need a husband as much as I need a wife…

The coward in her thought how much better this conversation with her dad would go if she had only said okay to Bo.

But that would've been ridiculous.

It would've been…

A most welcome solution?

Her dad said, "How was dinner?"

She held up the take-out box. "Good. I met Erika and brought back some ribs for us from the Shack." She resisted the urge to shift around, just as she used to the few times she'd gotten into trouble during her entire life.

"You left before you told me the exact date your fiancé's coming into town, Hol. I'd like to have a nice talk with him when he does get here."

Dad, don't even bother to prepare a speech.

That's what she should've said.

"He only told me it would be in a few weeks," she said, making sure her tone was nonchalant.

Deeper and deeper.

"He didn't even give you a date?" he asked.

"Please stop this, Dad. I feel like you think there wasn't any love involved with this baby—that what I have with the father is a tawdry thing."

Pressing her lips together, Holly made herself go quiet. Why had she blurted that out?

Because she, herself, doubted that Alan had ever felt any love?

Hank Pritchett glanced at Holly with some surprise. She *never* talked back.

"That's not what I intended to say," he said. "I only feel the urge to ask why your intended doesn't seem to care enough right now to be here."

At least it sounded as if her father been doing some thinking and accepting while she'd been gone. Apparently, he'd even transferred his anger from her to this fictional fiancé. In a way, that made Holly feel even worse, as if she'd gotten away with something.

Her father added, "I don't like any man who goes

off on a business trip instead of being with his pregnant girlfriend."

Well, then, he would've just *loved* Alan.

"I understand," she said, coming to sit next to him on the settee. "But, Dad, this baby is the best thing that's ever happened to me. I'm happy. Isn't that what you've always wanted for me?"

His blue eyes strayed to her stomach, and all Holly wanted was to have her dad take part in that happiness. The baby was a miracle, even if Alan hadn't been.

Her dad's gaze turned wistful, and he smiled as he looked at his future grandchild, although she suspected he was fighting the gesture.

"I call him or her Hopper," she said.

"You don't know what it is yet?"

"I know my baby's not an 'it,' that's for sure." She grinned. "We decided to wait on the 'he' or 'she' part until the birth." Well, *she'd* decided that. "The baby likes to move around inside me on occasion, like he or she is hopping around."

He clutched the afghan, as if sharing this moment with her mother. Holly's chest seemed to cave in. What she would give to have Mom here, too….

"When's Hopper coming?" he asked quietly.

She warmed at his use of the nickname, even if he'd sounded like he thought it was rather silly. "Two months."

"You hid him or her for a while."

"Yeah, I did."

But she wouldn't tell him why—about how she'd dreaded that look he'd leveled on her earlier, the frustration and disappointment of knowing she'd let him down.

Yet there was a way he *could* keep on believing that she was the golden girl he'd sent off to college....

She contained a buzz as she pictured Bo in the moonlight, trying to get her to accept his wacky proposal.

"So tell me about this fiancé," her father said.

Holly gulped. If she'd thought to avoid these questions, she'd thought wrong.

Deeper and even deeper...

She called upon the budding lawyer in her. Diversionary tactics.

First, she put the rib box near her dad, hoping the aroma would be enough to make his stomach grumble, but when he didn't bite, she gave in.

"He's in...business," she said.

Oh, so lame. She would have to do better than that.

Her dad wasn't nearly satisfied, either. "What kind of business?"

Desperate, she said the first thing on her mind. "Ranching."

Her father waited expectantly and, God help her, she could only think of Bo.

"He owns two spreads," she said, "but he's got other interests besides."

"Other interests?"

Deeper...

She stood from the settee, intending to go up to her room so she could this off for even one night longer. "If you don't mind, Dad, I'm really tired."

But he wasn't stopping. "This fiancé's sounding real shady to me. What's his name?"

All right, she was in a corner, anyway.

This was it—she would have to utter a fake name she'd already made up for just this sort of situation. She would have to commit herself and then suffer the consequences when this phantom fiancé never materialized.

Or she would have to get the truth over with right now.

It seemed like a thousand years went by as her dad sat on the edge of the settee like a predator ready to pounce on whatever came out of her mouth.

Just as Holly thought he was about to call her on her lies, her cell phone rang in the foyer, where she'd left it in the pocket of her coat.

She nearly jumped on her way to answer it.

"You get back here!" her dad said.

But she moved as fast as she safely could, shoved her hand into her coat pocket, pulled out her phone and said, "Hello?"

When she heard a familiar yet vexing voice, she didn't have it in her to be exasperated.

"Holly," Bo said, "don't hang up."

Everything came together for her in that moment, no matter how little sense it made in the real world—her sheer desperation for a way out, an easy, tempting answer.

The solution that'd been hanging in front of her, waiting for her to grab it.

"Hi, honey," she said.

There was a pause at the other end of the line.

"Where are you?" she continued.

Her dad's boot steps sounded on the planked floor, stopping just around the corner, where he leaned against the wall, his face red, his burly arms crossed over his chest.

Bo's tone was wary. "A few seconds ago, I would've said that you really wouldn't want to know where I am. I might've even said that you would've chewed me out for having the presumption to get your number, but—"

She cut him off with a smitten laugh, just for her father's sake. "I just want to know when you're going to get here," she said, smiling at her dad and pointing at the phone. *See, Dad, instant fiancé!* "Will it be more than the few weeks you told me you'd be gone?"

She couldn't leave any more of a hint for Bo to play off of than that.

God help her.

When her dad left the foyer, clearly relieved that this fiancé was going to get to the ranch sooner or later for him to question, Holly slumped back against the door.

She was doing this.

Really doing it.

Bo seemed to know something was amiss, and he didn't skip a beat. "I can be there in a snap."

No turning back now.

"How much of a snap?" she asked.

The last sound she heard on the phone was Bo's low, devil-may-care laugh.

Then there was a knock on the door.

Holly hung up the phone just as her father came back into the foyer, as bewildered as she was.

With her head reeling—what was she going to tell her dad when he saw Bo the mayor candidate, who hadn't been out of town at all?—she opened the door.

And there he was—Bo Clifton in his cowboy hat, a gleam in his eyes, that killer smile on his face while he held open his arms for her.

"Sweetheart," he said.

Feeling herself sliding down the rabbit hole, Holly said a rapid prayer and rushed to her "fiancé."

Chapter Three

As Holly nestled into Bo's arms, her blond curls tickled his face.

Honey. That's what she smelled like.

And her body…?

He felt every curve—the full breasts crushed against him, the lean muscles below her sweater.

The small swell of her baby bump.

Strangely touched, he backed away an inch, looked down at her, seeing how her cheeks flushed, her eyes shining with something between perplexity and…

Hell, he didn't know. But out of pure playfulness, he touched her cheek.

"Did you miss me?" he asked, just daring her to tell him why she'd changed her mind about his offer. Seeing how far she was willing to go now that he was here. He'd been just down the drive in the hopes that he could talk her into going out for a tea or whatever pregnant women drank, and the shorter the drive to her door, the less time she would have to change her mind about listening him out just one last time.

Sure, he was a little insistent, but Bo had always known when to go in for the kill, and Holly had sure seemed as if she'd been open to some more persuading back at the resort.

"I sure did miss you," she said, her voice thick with an emotion Bo couldn't name.

Obviously, she was acting the hell out of this.

But as he looked down at her, it felt real enough, awareness growing like a force field between them, urging him to lower his mouth to hers. Compelling him to.

Then her gaze went from a soft blue to an icy shade that told him she knew what kind of rascally thoughts he was thinking, and she pinched his waist under his coat, where her dad wouldn't be able to see it.

He let her go as she turned toward Hank Pritchett, but that certain something—that second of flickering fire—stayed with Bo, licking at his gut.

God knows why, because he hadn't chosen Holly as a true wife. Fire had no place here, just as it hadn't with his parents after a while.

"Dad," she said. "You know Bo Clifton."

Her father was a barrel of a man, and right now he had the complexion of a barrel made out of redwood as he stood in the foyer with his arms crossed. But even if Bo had known him for years and occasionally spoke to him around town, he wasn't about to act flippant with Hank, and he nodded respectfully to him.

As the older man seethed, Bo started to catch on to

the reason Holly had changed her tune about his offer. She'd been put into even more of a spot with her father, hadn't she? Why else would she have been so relieved to hear Bo on the phone? Why else would she have given him that enthusiastic hug at the door?

No matter right now. He would ask questions later and accept this boon from Holly.

"Sir," he said to Hank, recalling what Holly had told him on the phone about a three week absence and putting it together with all the information he'd culled from eavesdropping earlier. "Holly made me promise that she wasn't going to let you in on our secret until after the election, and it looks as if she made good on that."

Hank didn't seem to be hearing him. "Holly, you told me that your fiancé was out of town."

She clasped her hands, and Bo wondered if a woman with her steel would actually start wringing them.

He was all too glad to step in.

He rested his hand on Holly's back, felt her stiffen ever so slightly before she put that lovey-dovey smile back on her face and glanced at him with those big blue doe eyes.

"Hank," he said, "I know we've got a lot of explaining to do. But before we get into it, I want to let you know that I've been waiting far too long to get married to your daughter, and I intend to make her the happiest woman in the world."

With that, Bo motioned toward the parlor. Hank gave him a half-stink eye—a cautious glare, really—and disappeared behind the corner into the other room.

The second he was gone, Holly grabbed Bo's coat lapels, whispering, "I didn't give Dad a name for my fiancé…just said he owns two ranches and has varied business interests."

"Two ranches, huh?" Bo whispered back. "He sounds just like me."

"Don't get cocky." She narrowed her eyes. "And don't think I was modeling this fiancé after you or something."

"Why would I think that?"

Bo grinned, heading toward the parlor. When Holly began to follow, he held up a finger.

"I don't mind taking it from here."

She opened her mouth to protest, but Bo pressed his finger against her lips. He'd meant to do it out of more playfulness, but when her eyes widened and her mouth parted, a blast of desire singed him.

For a burning moment, he imagined bending just a few inches forward, closing the space between them, molding his lips to hers to see what it might feel like. How she might taste…

Hank's voice came from the parlor. "I ain't got all night."

It was as if Bo was a teenager who'd been caught in the backseat of a Cadillac with Hank Pritchett's daughter, and he stepped away from Holly. He recovered quickly though, doffing his coat and hat, handing them to her, then winking.

She rolled her eyes but didn't go anywhere, just waited while clutching his belongings.

When he arrived in the parlor, Hank was sitting before a fire, the orange light suffusing him, making him look even ten times hotter in the head than Bo would've liked.

Bo sat in a wingback chair opposite his future father-in-law's settee, but his rear had barely touched the seat before Hank drilled into him.

"You, of all men, Bo, taking advantage of Holly."

"Hank, I assure you—"

"Walking *out* on her."

"There was no walking, believe me. And definitely no running. Only a man out of his mind would let her go. I should explain why this situation seems out of sorts."

He paused, willing to let Hank get out more of his frustration before Bo segued into the next phase of persuasion—the part where he won over Holly's father.

When Hank didn't say anything more, Bo took that for a good sign, and off he went.

"While Holly was in Bozeman, at college, we ran into each other in town. I barely recognized her from years ago, but there she was, the most beautiful woman I'd ever seen." A whooping good start, and Bo realized that the telling of it wasn't hard in the least. All he had to do was recall earlier tonight, when he'd first seen Holly in the restaurant: blond curls, lively blue eyes—a woman he really did think to be beautiful.

"I was lost to her in that second," he added.

A lie, of course. But as something rotated in his chest, it felt as if it had really happened that way.

Hank had one hand buried in a varied-colored afghan, grasping it as if he might just be throwing a cushioned punch at Bo.

Time to explain more. "I knew right then that I had to spend the rest of my life with Holly."

"And what about her getting pregnant before you even brought her to the altar?"

Hank was leveling a death stare, and Bo had to remind himself that he wasn't the man who'd left Holly.

He was just the guy who was lying to her father now, although it was for a greater good.

It was for Thunder Canyon.

His mind whirred, spinning more story. "We kept our relationship quiet. Holly is discreet, as you know."

"Obviously," Hank said.

Stay on target. "Before we got pregnant, we'd been planning on getting married for months, but Holly wanted to finish school first. That was important to her—to finish what she'd started with her degree before embarking on a new stage in life, which we thought should include law school after we got settled. Those plans made sense to me, because she'd have to deal with finals and graduating, and adding all that wedding planning would've been far too much at that point."

Bo measured Hank's reaction, but the man hadn't moved a muscle, not even in his face.

So far, so good.

"Then I started thinking about running for mayor and she loved the idea. But you know Holly—she's the practical one. She added this to the pile of reasons to wait and announce our engagement. She said it would look better for me to be dating a graduate rather than a student." Bo lowered his voice, as if sharing a confidence with Hank. "She's been real sensitive about our age difference, and she believed that voters here in town might be the same."

Hank grunted, then said, "She's a decade or more younger than you. No one wants the kind of mayor who steals everyone's young daughters."

Okay, so he and Hank weren't quite there yet. But Bo understood. Holly's father was finding it tough to blame his daughter for this situation. She was Hank's little girl, and she always would be.

Bo got to the hardest part. "Then the baby came along."

He smiled like a happy father would, and, truthfully, Bo did have a soft spot for kids, so it wasn't a stretch. It was just that he hadn't ever thought he'd be the kind of man to have any children of his own—not with maintaining two ranches and having a pretty damned good time dating around. And certainly not with the example his parents had set with their divorce.

Then it hit him—he was going to be a father.

While the realization swam through his head, Bo felt Hank watching closely, so he got himself together.

"You also know how stubborn Holly is," he continued. "She insisted on a secret engagement while I ran for mayor. She didn't want Arthur Swinton to have a leg up in the campaign because she knew he'd twist the pregnancy into some kind of moral shortcoming for us, when that just isn't the case at all. She thought he'd turn everything into an ugly scandal and Thunder Canyon would come out the biggest loser in the end."

Hank looked into the fire. "Holly believes in you that much, does she?"

"Yes. But I didn't give up on changing her mind that easily. I wanted to shout out loud how we feel about each other because, surely, when the public could see how much I love her, they'd be just fine with voting for me, no matter what Arthur Swinton might say."

Hank exhaled, and suddenly, he seemed like an old man who'd been put out to pasture, unneeded, set aside. "I wish she'd at least told her father what was happening."

Bo came over to the settee, and it wasn't even because it was part of a plan to ingratiate himself with Hank. The guy just looked so sad.

"Holly relented tonight," Bo said, thinking Hank would like to hear this, even if the truth was being stretched. "She decided you should know after she saw how much it hurt you not to have known about the baby. She called me after she left the house, and I met her and Erika at the Rib Shack. She was only waiting until I got here to tell you everything."

"Even so..." Hank said, trailing off, still wounded.

"I've been counting down the days until I could finally do this the right way with Holly," Bo said. "That's why I came right over to ask you for her hand in marriage."

The older man looked away from the fire, and it was obvious that Bo had spoken to something within him.

Bo wasn't the cur who'd taken advantage of his daughter—not anymore. Bo might've even been on track to becoming a decent guy again in Hank's eyes.

"I'm going to love your daughter and our baby more than any man ever could," Bo said. "You can depend on that."

At least for six months....

Guilt tried to worm its way into Bo's gut, but he shut it out.

Still, when Hank gave a slow nod and glanced back into the fire while grasping that afghan, Bo didn't feel any sense of victory at all.

Around the corner, Holly nearly hugged the wall as she overheard the conversation.

I'm going to love your daughter and our baby more than any man ever could....

It should've been Alan the Rat saying those things to her dad.

But he'd never loved her, and she knew it. She'd ached for months after accepting that fact, too.

So why did it hurt so much to hear Bo in there talking to her dad now? Did the pain have something to do with how Bo sounded like he meant every last syllable, even though all of his promises were just as false as Alan's?

As Holly pushed herself away from the wall, she felt sick again. She rubbed her stomach, as if to show her baby that no matter what happened, Mommy would always, always be there for him or her, even without a father.

Meanwhile, Bo and her dad talked for a few more minutes, but Holly didn't really hear what they said. She just kept replaying the part about Bo vowing to love her and the baby.

But what if…?

Nah. She shouldn't go there, fantasizing, even for a second, that someone like Bo even had the capacity to utter these things to her and mean them.

She heard him say good-night to her father, then walk out of the parlor. When he rounded the corner, her pulse gave a jerk, then sputtered back to its normal cadence.

But when she looked into Bo's eyes, her heartbeat went full speed ahead.

She gestured for him to follow her to the kitchen, where they stood by counters littered with crumbs, unwashed plates and peanut butter and jelly jars with skewed lids. Her brothers had clearly been in here, too.

The stone hearth was dark, unlike the one in the

parlor. From the back of the cabin, she heard the door slam. Seconds later, she saw her father through the window, clad in his coat and cowboy hat. A sting of red light showed that he'd lit up a smoke.

Holly picked up a jar, screwing the lid on properly. "You're a magnificent storyteller."

He'd brought the rib box out of the parlor with him, and he put it in the fridge. "I had enough information to go off of, based on what I heard tonight and what I already know about you. And what people say here in Thunder Canyon about Holly Pritchett."

She didn't want to know what they said. All she cared about was her family. "How do you think it went?"

"He'll come around even more. He just needs some thinking time."

Bo fetched a couple of tin plates and put them in the sink. A guy who knew how to clean up. Little by little, he was racking up the points.

"And…?" she urged.

"Are you asking what happens next?"

He had that canary-eating grin again.

"I guess I am," she said, ignoring the lure of him. "I'm new to this faux-marriage drill, so I'm just not sure."

"Me, too, but we'll navigate it fine." He turned on the water to rinse the plates as she put the jelly and peanut butter jars in the pantry. "We'll have to set a date soon."

A date for the wedding.

Oh, this really was coming at her now…zooming… tearing up her head…

"I'd also appreciate it," Bo said, "if you'd start accompanying me on some campaign outings. Not too many. I don't want to tax you. But since our secret's going to be out in the open come tomorrow…"

She would have to think like the fake Holly now. She would have to remember how she and Bo had met as adults in Bozeman, just like he'd told her dad. She would have to call her college friends and give them that cover story about how she had fallen for Bo right after Alan had spurned her, and she'd been too embarrassed to admit to a rebound relationship to go public with it until now. She would have to act over the moon about this fiancé of hers.

Holly slid a glance to him as he used some liquid soap on the dishes. His thick blond hair was ruffled, giving him the impression of being groomed and a bit messy all at once. Somehow, that gave him a roguish air, and it tugged at her.

"Okay," she found herself saying. "I can do both of those things. Wedding date. Campaigning."

"We should lay out a deal, too—what's expected, not expected."

"Lay one out?" The imagery was more provocative than he'd probably intended.

"A deal. Lay out a deal."

Another amused grin. She was glad she was so entertaining.

"We already named a six month term," she said.

"We'll have to come to an agreement about the money I'll be giving you, too."

"I have a question about something else first." Here came the common sense part. "As far as this ruse goes, aren't you worried about what'll happen when you get married now, only to get an annulment a short time later? What will your constituents think of you then?"

Of course, Bo already had that covered, and his cocky stance showed it. "All I want to do is get elected. When the townsfolk see that I'm there for them, getting things done, keeping my campaign promises, they just might have sympathy for the both of us. They'll blame the failure of our marriage on all the work and long hours we've had to endure for the town's sake, but I'll take the brunt of any PR fallout beyond that."

"That's a risky strategy."

"I just need an opportunity to get into office, Holly. From there, I'll fly."

God help her, but she believed every word, yet that didn't mean she didn't have an even bigger concern. "Then there's acting like we're a real couple…."

He grin grew, and she knew just what he was thinking.

"There won't be any of that," she said.

"What?"

"You know what."

"Nookie?"

It was as if he'd shot her up with adrenaline, because it flew through her, making her heartbeat go on a rampage, stealing more of her breath.

Bo finished rinsing a plate, turned off the water and put the item in its drying rack. He leaned back against the counter, as casual as you please.

"There'll be no nookie, then."

She gave a clipped nod, doubting he would find her attractive, anyway, since she was swelling up a little more day by day, plus her stomach would no doubt be popping soon. She would be a beach ball, and although she didn't mind that at all, she wouldn't believe that a confirmed bachelor like Bo would be into it.

He grabbed a dishrag and wiped down the counter before she had a chance to.

"Tomorrow," he said, "some of my supporters are holding a rally in the resort's main parking lot. Two o'clock. Can you get out of work to be there?"

"I make my own hours with the online data entry, so it won't be a problem to show up."

He tossed the dishrag into the sink, then ambled toward her. Every one of her heartbeats seemed to stack themselves on top of the other, wobbling.

When he got within inches of her, she had no choice but to look up at him.

"Your dad," he murmured. "He's just outside and we're right in the line of his view, thanks to the window."

Was he hinting that they should kiss good-night, just for show?

Holly's lips warmed, electric with anticipation as he brushed his gaze over them.

A kiss.

She could practically imagine sinking against him, holding on to his shirt as he pressed his mouth against hers…

Getting control of herself, Holly moved away, heading toward the foyer. Behind her, she heard Bo chuckle, then follow.

She took his coat and hat from where she'd hung them on the foyer rack and handed them over. He put them both on.

Going to the door, he rested his hand on the knob. "By the way, I'll be bringing something to the rally that we'll need for you."

"What?"

"Just a minor detail."

Without further explanation, he opened the door, tipping his hat to her as he went outside and shut the door behind him, leaving Holly holding her breath and even more off balance than ever.

"You did *what?*" Erika said the next afternoon in the parking lot of the Thunder Canyon Resort.

The mountains loomed in back of her, just above the red-white-and-blue bunting that had been put up for the rally. A mostly young crowd wearing those Golden Days Ahead With Bo! cowboy hats and sweatshirts under thick coats had gathered, sporting signs for their candidate. Clouds hovered over the action, covering the sun.

Holly took Erika by the hand and led her to the outskirts of the festivities, near the edge of some pine trees.

Once there, Erika waited for Holly to explain, looking more than a little worried.

"I know," Holly said. "I can't believe I'm doing this. I spent all of last night tossing and turning, trying to figure out a better way. But there isn't one."

"Holly, I understand how it feels to be judged and how afraid you are to go through that with your family, but there's got to be another way."

"Well, it's too late now. This morning, my dad actually had a smile on his face, as if he'd thought about my engagement good and hard and he was starting to come to peace with it." Holly's chest seemed banded together. "Do you know how good that felt, to see him like that?"

"But it's based on a falsehood, Holly, and you're the

last person I ever thought who'd would be tangled up in such a web of them."

See, even her good friend held Holly to such standards that she wondered how she'd ever lived up to them in the first place.

Instead of facing the disappointment of failing Erika, too, Holly pulled her wool coat around her, glancing toward the rally, where Bo's campaign manager, an older, no-nonsense woman named Rose Friedel, was getting the action started.

Holly attempted another explanation for Erika's sake. "I think my head's not on right because of these pregnancy hormones."

Yeah—that had to be it. They'd mixed her up and shaken her around as good as any strange cocktail.

"Pregnancy hormones or not," Erika said, "you've still got time to back out of this deal."

"But—"

"But your father and family." Erika touched Holly's arm. "I'm here to tell you that what you saw on your dad's face yesterday when he found out about the baby will pale in comparison to what he's going to show you when this house of cards comes tumbling down. And it will tumble, Holly."

Holly nudged the dirt with the toe of her boot. She wished Erika could've seen how Bo had so deftly handled her father, how he'd whipped up a solid story that covered her.

How he'd wooed her dad as surely as he wooed everyone else.

"And what if we *could* pull it off?" she asked.

Erika groaned.

Holly's voice gained strength. "What if six months

come and go and no one is any wiser or the worse for this temporary masquerade?"

Erika started to leave. Then she seemed to reconsider, turning back to Holly long enough to lower her voice and say, "I'm going to stand by you, whatever you decide to do. But I wish you would think this through a lot more."

She walked toward the rally, where Holly knew Erika's for-real fiancé, Dillon Traub, was waiting.

Yes, Erika was going back to a reality that Holly could only hope for, because her own was about as true as a three-headed moose.

As her friend disappeared into the crowd, a shiver traveled through Holly.

It was as if…

She looked toward the entrance to the resort, and there he was, near the elegantly rustic building's entrance, apart from everyone else.

Bo..

He'd just emerged from the five-story central wing, dressed unlike any politician she'd ever seen, in his jeans, boots, sheepskin coat and that cowboy hat.

He'd seen her first, and she had no idea how long he'd been watching her. But just the very idea that she'd been in his sights sent a thrill through Holly, head to toe.

He sauntered toward her and, suddenly, she had no idea what to do with herself. Maybe pick this imaginary piece of fuzz off her coat. Maybe pretend as if she was terribly interested in the rally.

Still time to back out of this deal…

But when Bo came to stand in front of her, all of Erika's guidance spiraled away, and Holly smiled up at him, unable to stop herself.

Her fiancé.

Committed, for better or worse.

"You ready?" she asked, hoping he hadn't heard the tiny tremble in her voice.

"Just about." He dipped a hand into his coat pocket, fisting it around something he didn't yet reveal.

Then he reached out and clasped one of her hands in his.

Warm. So warm.

It took her a moment to realize that he had taken out a ring, and she gasped.

This was what he'd meant by bringing her a "detail" for their ruse. She hadn't even thought about a ring, only concentrating on the business parts, like when the wedding should be and where.

The diamond sparkled. Simple and elegant, just the sort of ring she would've picked out for herself.

"My grandmother left it to me before she passed on," he said.

His *grandmother's* ring?

"Bo, you can't use this. It's almost a slap in her face."

"She would've approved of what I want to do for Thunder Canyon. Grams was practical like that. Kind of like you, too."

He slipped it onto Holly's finger, taking their charade a dangerous step further.

As she admired the alluring gleam of it, she couldn't speak. That's when the tears would come, and she wouldn't waste them on a semi-proposal that shouldn't hold any meaning. She would be giving this ring back soon enough.

But, in the meantime, it didn't hurt to run her thumb

against the back of the gold band, didn't hurt to get used to the foreign feel of it circling her finger.

She glanced up at Bo only to find him staring at the ring, too, an unreadable expression on his face.

Then, as if he wanted to hide what he was thinking, he grinned.

"I'm all set," he said, taking her by the hand. "Are *you* ready for this?"

No welching once she came out from under these pines and into that rally.

In her tummy, her baby gave a healthy kick, as if goading Holly.

Baby.

This was all about what her child would need.

"Ready," Holly said.

And they walked out into the open together.

Chapter Four

The crowd at the rally had loved the first part of Bo's speech, and their cheers were just coalescing into a chant—*"Bo! Bo! Bo!"*—when his campaign manager subtly tapped her watch from the sidelines, near a barricade of pickup trucks that his volunteers had used to haul their equipment to the resort.

Based on Rose's gesture, it was nearly time to go into the main lodge to meet a reporter for coffee and an interview, during which Bo intended to give out more details about his and Holly's engagement and pregnancy. It would be a "tell-all" exclusive Bo hoped would cover most of their bases.

But before he even got to that, he needed to lay the groundwork for those explanations to his supporters. Rose knew all about his intentions, and she'd planned today's strategy like a four-star general.

Bo held up his hands, asking for quiet, and the chanting faded. Then he wrapped it up.

"I've talked about change a lot during this campaign, and I imagine you can recite most of what I've said based on repetition," he said into his microphone.

The crowd laughed. One man even shouted, "We'll still listen, Bo!"

More laughter. Applause.

Bo grinned, then got a little more serious. "I've presented plans for drawing in new customers from out of town for our small businesses. I've practically chatted a mile-long streak about improving our infrastructure and education." He paused, looking into as many faces as he could—seeing the hope in their eyes, the trust they were putting into him.

He clutched the microphone, vowing not to let any of them down.

"We can go so many places together, because this town has been successful in the past. Gold wasn't the only reason Thunder Canyon found itself in the flush—we were on top because of our people."

A few cheers. The beginning of more applause, which grew moment by moment as Bo raised his voice over it.

"The *citizens* are the town's best natural resource, and we can raise Thunder Canyon back to its former greatness if we mine what's within ourselves. It'll take work—I won't fool you about that—and it'll take everyone working *together,* but we can prosper again, folks. We can do it."

As the crowd erupted into a full-fledged cheer, he lowered the mic, his gaze seeking out the one face that inspired him the most.

Near his campaign manager, Holly was raptly watching Bo, her hands clasped against her chest, as if she'd stopped applauding so she could hear him better. Somehow, her approval infused him with more optimism.

So did the sight of that diamond ring, flashing from her finger.

Right now, everything seemed just as it should be, and caught up in the moment, Bo crooked his finger to her, asking her to join him.

Her lips parted, and she didn't move.

Had she changed her mind?

Panic struck Bo as all his dreams tumbled by: getting Thunder Canyon on its feet again. Bringing back those days of sunshine and hope he'd felt back when he'd been just a kid, before his introduction to the darkness life could bring, when his uncle had been murdered.

But Bo could do something about all of that now, even if years had gone by and he was getting a late start. He could make a difference, clean up the world one little space at a time, and his marriage to Holly would pave the way for that.

His supporters had quieted, waiting for his next sentence, but Bo just looked at Holly.

Come on, he thought. *Help me out here.*

She touched her stomach, as if reminding herself of what their marriage would provide.

Then, as his heart pounded, she made her way to him.

He could see his campaign manager clapping; Rose was in on the ruse, so she was encouraging Holly. Then the older woman winked at him, clearly relieved that things were rolling along.

As Holly came closer, Bo bounded over to meet her, taking her hand in his, escorting her to the limelight.

He squeezed her hand, speaking into the mic again.

"I've talked about change, all right. And I'm going to show you that I'm not just *all* talk."

When he put his arm around Holly, she seemed cautious at first, until he rubbed her shoulder, acting the part of the loving fiancé. As she leaned into his side, Bo flashed a captivated smile down at her.

Holly returned it, and the crowd roared.

They liked her—liked *them*.

He waited until they'd calmed down before he went on.

"Several months ago," he said, "I found a woman who changed me in a lot of ways. And as you bachelors out there know, change doesn't come easy."

A few hoots from Thunder Canyon's single-and-loving-it contingent.

"But," Bo added, "it's a perfectly welcome matter when you fall for a woman as amazing as Holly Pritchett."

The response was deafening, and Bo had to shout over them. "She finally allowed me to announce our wedding!"

With that, a flood of flashbulbs enveloped them, and they posed for pictures, waving at the audience. Rose turned on the stereo speakers, filling the atmosphere with a lively Charlie Daniels fiddle tune that made the supporters clap in time while most of them turned to each other, already asking questions, trying to work out the whats-whos-and-whys of his stunning announcement. He and Holly kept waving as they left the stage, from where Bo had planned to make their way to the resort, which wasn't more than two hundred feet away.

He held on to Holly as the people surrounded them, offering congratulations, asking about the engagement.

"You'll read all about it come tomorrow morning's edition of the paper!" Bo said.

Everyone kept a respectful distance, just as Bo knew the good people of Thunder Canyon would, but he started feeling real protective of Holly, anyway. He gathered her closer until they got into the main lodge, which boasted a huge open lobby, with voices echoing from the ceiling three stories up. A freestanding fireplace, leather sofas and a life-size elk sculpture dominated the area, but before Bo got to any of it, three hardy, blond men caught up to him and his fiancée.

Holly's older brothers.

The two eldest, Hollis and Nick, resembled their little sister the most, except that they had a whole lot more testosterone and blue-eyed fervor.

"You gone crackers?" Hollis asked, guiding Holly away from Bo as if she'd been kidnapped by him. "All three of us got voice mails from you late last night, and we've been trying to get ahold of you this morning."

"I meant to talk to you boys at length, but as you can see, things have been a little busy for me."

"Dad filled us in," Hollis continued, "but he couldn't explain what's gotten into you."

Holly extricated herself from her oldest brother.

Good God—she hadn't talked to the Pritchett boys one on one before this? No wonder they were steamed.

But Bo could guess why she'd decided to leave late-night messages; judging from her brothers' responses now, they would've gone ballistic, and she'd wanted to put it off, jumping headfirst into this ruse without anyone to stop her.

Dean, the youngest, had deep green eyes, plus a darker shade of blond hair, which was clipped more closely to his head than the others. "You're acting like you didn't think we'd have any kind of reaction to this news."

"I expected maybe a congratulations and a hug," Holly said. "Not a stampede."

Nick was the stockiest of the lot, just like a bull who had it in mind to perhaps run a new member of the family over.

"What's this all about, Bo?" he asked.

Although Bo suspected he was only moments away from getting the tar beat out of him, he didn't overreact. Hell, he didn't even have much of a chance to say anything before Holly went toe-to-toe with Nick.

"Just calm down and stop embarrassing me," she said.

Every one of the brothers seemed to go red to some degree or another.

Bo stepped in. "Listen, we'll sort this out. After all, you men know me. Am I the type who'd set out to corrupt Holly, especially knowing I'd have *you* to contend with?"

Hollis frowned. "I recall a Bo Clifton who seemed to enjoy quite a bit of female companionship in the past, and I'm not sure I like that he's enjoyed my sister."

All the brothers had probably heard about his track record. It wasn't that Bo was a tomcat, exactly. It was just that…

Well, he was still young, and he'd never really

intended to settle down. Hadn't made a secret of that either.

Behind them, the doors opened, and Rose Friedel walked into the lobby, her bobbed gray hair as sleek as her deep purple suit. She tapped that watch of hers and headed toward the elk sculpture, where they were to meet Mark Anderson, who owned *The Thunder Canyon Nugget* and had taken it upon himself to report this particular story—a headline grabber.

"I'll tell you what," Bo said to the brothers. "I've got an appointment right now, and it won't take but an hour. Why don't you three meet me at the lounge then? I'll answer any questions you have. And open up a bar tab while you're at it—it's all on me."

Holly gave Bo a glance that told him she would do damage control until he got there.

He braved the wrath of the Pritchett boys and rested a hand on her shoulder. He'd only meant to give her another one of those charade-driven, loving looks he'd bestowed on her out at the rally, but this time…

This time he found himself doing it with real feeling.

Eyes so blue that he felt himself falling into the wells of them…

Just as Bo's blood began to bubble in his veins, Nick took it upon himself to interrupt, his tone much milder than it'd been previously.

"All right, Bo," he said. "We'll be waiting for you there."

With some difficulty, Bo pulled his gaze away from Holly to see that the brothers were watching him with odd expressions. Confusion, which would surely lead to understanding once Bo took up where this look had left off and assured them of his "feelings" for Holly.

As the Pritchett boys headed for the lounge upstairs, Bo thought that he and his bride had cleared this latest obstacle pretty well.

"I hope you brought ketchup," Holly said when her brothers were out of earshot.

"What?"

"They want to eat you alive, so you might as well dish yourself up properly."

"Nah." Across the lobby, which wasn't nearly as filled with guests as it'd been in the good old days, Rose was greeting Mark Anderson. "If your brothers were going to kill me, they'd have just done it right here."

"I'll stay during your meeting with them so no one—not even Nick and his hot head—will mess with you."

She looked so protective of *him* now, with her hands fisted at her sides. It tweaked something in Bo, but he passed it off as gratefulness for her loyalty.

"Though I appreciate it," he said, "I've got it handled."

Holly let out a long sigh, as if she was just as exasperated with him as she'd been yesterday, when he'd first approached her with this whole business. She glanced around the lobby, her gaze landing near the fireplace, where Erika Rodriguez had come inside to visit with Erin Castro, whom most people considered to be the town's woman of mystery. Bo didn't know her well, but he'd heard that she'd moved here recently, and had just been hired on as a permanent receptionist by the resort.

His political instincts went into overdrive. Maybe he would speak to Rose about asking Erin Castro to be a part of his campaign—a newcomer who'd appreciated Thunder Canyon so much that she'd decided to stay. She was the perfect example of what this town needed to do—attract more people, build itself up again.

Then Dillon Traub joined Erika and Erin, bringing them each a paper cup of coffee. Erika kissed her new fiancé on the cheek, and they stared into each other's eyes for a moment that seemed to span an eternity.

Love, Bo thought. That's what it truly looked like.

But what would happen on down the line, after they'd lived with each other for years? After they'd both changed, just as his parents had done?

And how would it be between them when their differences became so pronounced that they couldn't stand one another anymore…?

Because that's what love was to Bo—maybe it was real for a time, but it would never last.

Holly stirred next to him. From the thoughtful expression she wore, she'd been keying in on Erika and Dillon, too.

Was she thinking that she was watching two people who'd genuinely found their soulmates? That she wished it'd been that way for her with the father of her baby?

Anger at the man—or *less* than a man—dogged Bo. He wanted to wring that Alan's neck for messing with Holly and stranding her child.

But Bo was going to make up for it.

He touched Holly's cheek. It was still a little cold from being outside, and he wished he could be enough to warm it.

When she flushed, as if his touch meant more than he'd intended, he lowered his hand.

What had he been thinking?

She moved away from him, heading toward the stairs and the lounge, where her brothers were waiting. "I'll keep the boys at bay for now and leave you alone with them when you get there."

He gave her his trustworthy grin. "After you go, I'll be off to campaign headquarters. I'll call from there to let you know I survived."

"No, I think I'll come by, just to see you with my own eyes." She stuck her hands into her coat pockets. "Besides, we've got a lot more to talk about."

Indeed. Wedding plans and beyond.

And it seemed as if every bit of it had already started to fill her head while she smiled, almost as if to herself. Then she gave him a tiny wave before she went to the lounge.

Bo watched her go, enjoying her walk, her sense of grace that made her stand out even in a room full of people.

Then he continued his campaign, heading toward the reporter.

Holly arrived at town square a couple hours later, shortly before sunset. She walked to an abandoned storefront, the old sign that still read Dilly's hovering over a temporary banner that practically shouted Bo's campaign mantra.

He'd set up shop in a former drugstore where everyone used to go for malts until the economy had forced an early retirement on Tucker and Addie Dillinger. Inside, the marble counters still remained intact, though they were now covered with pamphlets that volunteers put together as they sat on the stools. In red-upholstered booths, more Bo Believers talked on cell phones to constituents who needed some convincing that Bo was their man. Emptied shelves held posters, signs, hats and T-shirts.

Holly discovered Bo in a glassed-in, closed-door office near the back of the place, where he huddled with Rose behind an old desk. He and his campaign manager looked like polar opposites—Bo with his cowboy gear, Rose dressed in a crisp business suit and her get-to-the-point sophisticated bob.

Holly knocked on the door, and they glanced up from the laptop computer they'd been using.

Bo smiled, and it was the same as always—as if he'd reserved a certain happiness for her and her only.

Right.

"There she is," he said once she'd entered the room.

"Hi." A whole flock of hummingbirds had taken wing in her stomach, fluttering like mad.

She ignored that, holding up a writing notebook she'd brought with her. "Ready to get down to it?"

Rose stretched her lean arms above her head. Holly could almost imagine her wheeling and dealing and darting around at the PR firm she'd been said to work at before Bo had recruited this family friend.

"Wedding plans?" she asked Holly.

"I thought it'd be a good idea to get on them as soon as possible."

"You bet." Rose wandered away from Bo. "We were just wrapping up for the day."

Holly slid into a chair in front of the desk. She felt the brush of Bo's gaze all over her, and she wished he would stop it. They didn't have to playact so much in front of

Rose—Bo had sent her a text message last night telling Holly that his campaign manager knew everything.

As the older woman went to the door, she said, "I like the notion of a Wild West themed wedding, myself. It suits Thunder Canyon and would catch the interest from Swinton's crowd, especially."

"Sounds fun," Holly said. Not her idea of a dream wedding, but, hey, she could adapt, just as long as she could choose her own dress. That's really what mattered to Holly; unlike most women, she'd always just pictured the gown, and everything around it was lower on the list of wedding happiness.

"Would it be okay," Rose said, "if I contacted an old friend who'd do a bang-up job of planning? She retired a few years ago, but I'm sure she'd be more than happy to have one last crack at it. Believe you me, she's a miracle worker. With her dedicated help, we could whip up an event by next weekend."

Next weekend?

This was Friday.

"Wow," Holly said, because her brain had just been fried.

"We need to step on it before the election," Rose said.

"Sure. Next weekend is great." Holly sloughed off her coat and let it hang on the back of her chair. "I guess I should put my energies into finding a dress and rounding up a guest list then? I have college friends who'll need a few days to get over the shock of my romance."

That is, after Holly even told them about it.

She would have to do some smooth Bo-type talking to unruffle their feathers, because they wouldn't be happy that she'd kept them in the dark about her love affair with Bo. But having her friends at the wedding would only add to the validity of their story.

Jeez, she thought. More and more lies.

Where would they stop?

"That would be fantastic," Rose said. "But you can leave the rest to me."

As the woman shut the door, Holly thought the assurances seemed all too familiar.

She turned to Bo. "'Leave the rest to me.' Sounds like something you told me earlier, when you said you'd take care of my brothers. So how did the gladiator training go?"

Bo leaned back in his chair, resting his hands on the back of his head. Confident.

Scamp.

"Would it irritate you if I said that you shouldn't worry about a thing?"

Holly laughed. "Actually, I'm glad to hear that."

"Your brothers aren't exactly pussycats to deal with, but they mellowed after I explained about how much I adore you and the baby."

Taking that in stride, Holly opened the notebook, which she'd started maintaining back when she'd thought she'd fancied getting married to Alan. She scanned the ideas she'd scribbled down for a wedding, but unlike the file she'd kept for wedding dress clippings, it was nothing detailed.

Family only, small. On the ranch, rose trellises. Simple, elegant.

But she was game for a Wild West blowout, too, if that's what would work for Bo.

Still, Holly didn't cross out her ideas. It seemed like

that would only erase a true wedding from her heart, and maybe someday, there'd still be a chance...

She set down the notebook. Her chances had probably already passed her by, and she should consider herself lucky that Bo had come along to help her out.

"Seriously," Bo said. "Your brothers got that murderous gleam out of their eyes, but their bruised egos could use a bit more appeasing. They said they'd be at the ranch tonight."

"They're there more often than not to raid the pantry. Why shouldn't they take the opportunity to razz lil' sis as much as they can at the same time?"

"They love you, Holly."

"Yeah, they really do." She plucked a pen from the leather holder on his desk. "And I pretty much love them."

When she grinned at Bo, she made it clear that her brothers were the end-all-be-all. She would go mountain lion on anyone she believed was taking advantage of *them,* so she couldn't stay mad at the boys for giving Bo a hard time today.

"Want me to drop you off tonight?" he asked, "just so I can stick around and see how it goes?"

His caring tone wrapped around her. She'd never heard such a thing from Alan.

"Don't you worry about a thing, Bo."

They settled down to talk about plans, deciding to hold the wedding at his ranch, the Rockin' C. But when it came time to talk about a full-fledged honeymoon trip, they decided to "put it off" until after the birth of the baby and some months after. Of course, by then, the marriage would be over. As for living arrangements, she would have to move into his home after the wedding, just to give credence to their relationship.

"But separate bedrooms, right?" she asked.

"I've got a few to spare."

She wrote that down, but when she glanced up at him again, she found him watching her in a way that made her think he could talk her into sharing a bed if he wanted it. That, if they stepped over a line, this wouldn't be a lie at all.

Her mind—and libido—wandered. What would it be like with Bo?

A sigh wound through her, running like a silken thread, taut and ready to break…

He stood from his chair, destroying the spell.

Had he felt it, too?

"Hot chocolate." There was grit in his voice as he went for his coat and hat on a rack by the door.

Hot what?

Then he grabbed her coat from the back of her chair. "Or coffee. I need caffeine, since it's going to be a long night for me. Maybe some decaf tea for you."

He held open her coat and she slipped into it. Before she could thank him, he was out the door.

The volunteers greeted him, their workstations strewn with pizza boxes, Chinese food or take-out cartons from the Hitching Post. He opened the door for Holly, and once she stepped out, the fall air pressed against her cheeks.

"Getting colder by the night," she said, hoping small talk would cut the sudden awkwardness.

"We can go to a café, where it's warmer inside."

"No, this is beautiful." She smelled the wood smoke on the air, looked at the sunset colors painting the wide sky. "There's a cart in the town square where we can grab that coffee and tea. It should still be open."

They went in that direction and arrived within a minute. He paid for their drinks and they found a bench under an oak, with all its autumn leaves swaying with the help of a small breeze that came and went.

"Do you go stir-crazy a lot in that office?" she asked.

The coffee cup was halfway to his mouth and he stopped it there.

"I mean," she continued, "you seemed to want to get the heck out of Dodge pretty quickly tonight."

He took a gulp of the coffee, then nodded. "You got me. Being at that desk was riding on my nerves. I'm not one who can sit still for long."

"I'm sure we'll keep you running as mayor of this place."

"From your mouth to God's ears," he said.

She wanted to ask him if he'd also jumped out of his office chair because of that moment between them. The tension that had just about split the room in two.

But she didn't dare. Those darn pregnancy hormones—they were making her imagine things. They were making her want when she shouldn't be wanting.

As if responding to that, a kick thumped in her belly, and she sucked in a breath, her hand going to her tummy.

"You okay?" Bo asked.

"Yes." She patted her stomach. "It's Hopper."

"The baby. What's—"

"Nothing's wrong. He or she just decided it'd be a good time to give me a boot, that's all. I've got an active one."

His gaze dwelled on her midsection. Holly had spent so long hiding her condition that, now, she only wanted to let the town see that she was about to give birth to the biggest blessing she'd ever received.

And she was free to show everyone that, wasn't she?

"Here," she said, unbuttoning her coat and taking Bo's hand, guiding it to her bump. "Let's see if the baby goes for it again."

Bo laughed, and there was a nervous edge to it, as if he'd never thought to find himself cupping a woman's pregnant belly.

After a second passed with no action, he said, "You're still pretty small for seven months."

"I don't show much. It's my slender build, the doctor says. I'll be seeing her next week for another appointment."

A heartbeat clomped by. Two.

"After the wedding," she added.

The baby kicked, and Bo hooted.

"There's a boy!" he said.

"Or girl. I don't know which one yet. I decided that I wanted to wait and see until the baby is born."

He nodded, going along with her decision, but he didn't remove his hand. Holly didn't remind him that he should, either. It just felt so nice, sitting here in the town she'd grown up in, finally a part of it when she'd feared that she would be cast out only a day ago.

She realized that she'd even put her hand on top of his, her palm mapped over his skin. He seemed to become aware of it at the same time she did, and he slightly moved his hand on her belly.

"Bo…?" she said, not knowing what she was going to ask.

Before he answered, a flash went off, startling her, blinding her vision, even as Bo took his hand away and got up from the bench. She was still recovering as Bo asked whoever had taken the picture to leave them some privacy.

Even when Holly's vision finally colored up again, she found that it hadn't cleared much at all.

Not when it came to Bo.

Chapter Five

The clouds were still around to cover the sun the next morning as Bo went to the ROOTS storefront building to meet Holly for another interview he'd arranged, this time with the new online department of *The Thunder Canyon Nugget.*

The newspaper had sent a fresh-from-college blogger who was building up the Internet aspect of the business, and when they arrived at ROOTS, Bo paused before the door. The spiky-haired kid, Jerry Farina, photographed him, just as he'd done last evening in the square, while he'd been doing some preliminary research and come upon Bo and Holly there.

But when his camera flashed this time, Bo only remembered how Holly had flinched at that photo last night, when they'd been having a private moment in the park, his hand cradling her belly.

He shook it off and said, "You know much about ROOTS, Jerry?"

"Sure." The blogger adjusted his digital camera. "Haley Anderson started it, wanting to 'pay it forward' in her community, especially with a younger crowd who needs a little more TLC than your average bears. It's the most popular with high school students—they like to come here to socialize—and the mentors are around to help with homework or even just to talk."

Jerry took another picture. "How many hours will Holly be putting in here, with her condition and all?"

Bo had been trying to take the temperature of the town ever since the news had hit about Holly's pre-wedding pregnancy this morning in the newspaper. He was pretty sure the younger citizens, like Jerry, were taking it well, but he was just waiting for Swinton's response, plus that of the more conservative citizens of Thunder Canyon.

"Holly's going to need some rest, so she'll be letting up on the volunteering soon," Bo said. "But if she had her way, she'd be bustling around Thunder Canyon minutes before *and* after the birth."

Then Bo quietly opened the door, revealing a mellow, Saturday-morning scene inside the storefront. About seven teens were here already, lounging on the sparse selection of thrift-store furniture. Most were watching cartoons on the TV. One redheaded girl in hipster braids was playing a game on her cell phone while leaning against the wall that'd been painted with Haley Anderson's mural, which featured images like iPods, purses, footballs and other assorted teen paraphernalia.

Across the room, Carleigh Benedict, who'd been running ROOTS since Haley had gotten engaged to Marlon

Cates and celebrated by taking a long trip with him, glanced up from the computer table. She was sitting with a boy wearing braces, and she smiled at Bo and Jerry. Bo waved back, keeping silent so as not to disturb the peace.

He continued searching the room, although he didn't admit to himself who he was looking for until he actually found her.

Holly.

She stole a breath out of him without even trying. All she was doing was sitting in a corner with a ponytailed brunette girl, obviously coaching the teen on writing an essay or letter. Holly was murmuring, maybe in encouragement, as she pointed something out in the teen's notebook.

When the girl's face lit up, as if a light bulb had gone on in her brain thanks to Holly's guidance, his fiancée smiled.

How was it that a woman who'd found herself in such a fix still had time to help others...and to take such joy in it?

Bo glanced at the other kids—every one of whom would rather be here on a Saturday morning than at home with their families. They all seemed alone in some way, just as he'd felt after the murder of his uncle. Bo had been older than these guys when it'd happened—fresh out of college, just like Holly—but the event had changed Bo's perception of everything.

His family hadn't been able to comfort him since they were grieving, too, and Bo wished there'd been a place like ROOTS back then, for him and his cousins and Stephanie Julen, whose father had been killed with Uncle John. He wished there'd been people like Holly…

Jerry the blogger took a picture of the mural, and the redheaded girl moved away from it, shooting Jerry one of those teenaged annoyed faces that could make even an adult cringe. Bo smiled at her in apology for ruining her game on the cell phone, and she glanced at him with interest, as if recognizing him, before returning to her pursuits.

The flashbulb had caught Holly's attention, and when she saw Bo, there was…something about her.

A spark?

A smile that had grown even bigger?

Whatever it was, she tamed it into what Bo recognized to be that "fiancée smile" as he went over to offer a hand as she stood from the floor.

Jerry didn't waste a second—he captured a photo of the "happy couple." Holly withstood it like a trouper.

"Ms. Pritchett," the blogger said, "is now a good time to ask you a few questions?"

"About ROOTS? Certainly."

Bo almost chuckled. She'd made it clear that personal questions about the pregnancy and their engagement—topics that had already been covered in this morning's edition of the newspaper—were off-limits.

The perfect mayor's wife—gracious yet strong.

Holly linked her arm through Bo's. "If you'll just give me a minute?"

"No problem." Jerry wandered away, stopping at the mural to get a better view of the details.

Holly glanced at the girl she'd been mentoring, but the teen was writing like a dervish, the tip of her tongue sticking out as her pen flew across the page.

They moved away from her and into a private corner near the front window.

"You must've gotten here early," he said.

"I did some of my data entry work at the crack of dawn so I could be here for Tatiana." Holly indicated the writing teen. "She's working on her college application and says she wants to be a lawyer, just like I..."

Holly stopped, but Bo could guess what she'd been about to say.

Just like I'd wanted to be.

Bo didn't even check himself as he used a finger to tip up her chin. "You can still do anything you want."

"I'm going to be pretty busy with a baby for the next few years."

She hadn't included him in that statement. But why should she?

Bo shifted while surprising guilt gnawed at him. "Speaking of the data entry, are you going to give notice? You don't need to work anymore."

She opened her mouth, as if to protest, but closed it, merely nodding. He could tell Miss Independent here was just getting used to the notion of taking money from him, that it ripped her up to have to take anything from anybody.

Maybe she needed to know that he didn't think of her as some charity case—she was worth a lot, and not just to him...

Or more to the point, to his campaign.

"Being at ROOTS," he said, "and seeing you in action just reminds me of why I want to be mayor. There are people behind every policy, and the kids here are just a peek into that."

"Community," she said. "That's what ROOTS is

about. That's what can solve so many things. If people just stopped talking about what's wrong and got something started like Haley did..."

There was real conviction in her tone, and Bo fed off of it.

As the flashbulb went off from Jerry's camera again, Holly gave Bo a jaded look, and if he said so himself, jaded didn't belong on Holly, even if she *was* thinking about how Bo was treating this as a photo op.

He was talking before he could stop himself. "Publicity's not why I'm here."

It was really about the people of Thunder Canyon, not his ego or because he liked being in the newspaper. But it sure seemed like that was the case right now.

Bo girded himself against that. To win, he needed publicity. So why deny it?

Jerry started to meander back over to them. Bo tucked a curl behind Holly's ear, not for show, but because she'd seen Jerry coming and she hadn't exactly seemed delighted about it.

Buck up, he thought to her.

As if hearing that, she put on her game face.

"Grant and Steph are coming to my place for dinner tonight," he said. "You up to it?"

"I'd love to be there. I've just got a gown fitting this afternoon, then, I suspect, a nap."

"If dinner's going to tire you out..."

"I've been having an easy pregnancy, and that shouldn't change in the space of an afternoon. I'll be there."

The way she said it made things clear: dinners and appearances were a part of their deal.

But that wasn't why Bo wanted her to be with him tonight.

Was it?

An hour later, as Bo sat at his desk in his campaign office, Rose Friedel closed the door behind her while holding up this morning's edition of *The Thunder Canyon Nugget.*

"Perfect," she said, tossing the copy at him.

He caught it, seeing the front-page picture of him and Holly at the rally, along with the headline Bo's Already Struck Gold!

He set down the paper. "I read it. It's a fair enough piece."

"Mark asked you some very direct questions about the pregnancy, and you rose to the occasion, Bo. Good job."

He'd told the journalist that he and Holly had always been as good as married. And, late last night, when Mark had called Bo for a few follow-up questions before the paper went to press, he'd asked him to comment about Swinton's reaction to Bo's announcement.

"This is what your opponent told me," Mark had said over the phone. "'No surprise. We just have new proof that Bo Clifton's wild days really aren't behind him. He couldn't even contain himself with a good girl like Holly Pritchett. To me, that doesn't show a lot of self-control, and we need that in a mayor.'"

The older man even had the *conjones* to hint about the age difference between bride and groom, just as Holly had anticipated.

But Bo's responses to the newsman had subtly painted

Swinton as a judgmental man who was frighteningly behind modern times.

Now, as he kept his hand on the paper, he said, "We'll see what Swinton comes up with next, Rose. Based on what he said to Mark, it almost seems as if the guy's just daring me to go through with this marriage, and I'm not even going to flinch."

"Daring you to go through with it? That part might be all in your mind." Rose sat on the cusp of his desk, the purple jacket of one of her many pantsuits brushing the surface.

Bo glanced at that picture of him and Holly. If he didn't know any better, he would've sworn that he was the happiest man on earth. "Ironic, huh? Every promise I've made about helping Thunder Canyon is no lie, but when it comes to my private life, everything's falser than a wooden nickel."

Rose grabbed the paper, turning it to the gossip section. There, the picture that'd been taken last night by Jerry the blogger—the photo of Holly and Bo in the park—stood out like a ringing shout.

Bo could hardly believe it was him, touching Holly's stomach so tenderly, an expression of wonderment on his features. The caption read A Private Moment for the Candidate.

Then there was Holly's face.

As her hand covered his, it seemed like she'd been just as moved as Bo had been.

"If you ask me," Rose said, "that's no wooden nickel."

Bo calmly folded up the paper, tucking it to the side of his desk. "Stop romanticizing this."

"Oh, no romance from me, my friend. You just might

need to be reminded that there's a line here, and you don't want to cross it."

"I won't."

"You're getting awfully close, judging by that photo."

Rose got up from his desk and opened his door, letting in the sounds of cell phones ringing, volunteers chatting to the community and dashing around the room with newly printed fliers.

"I know what my priorities are," he told his manager. "And I'll damned well maintain them."

Rose paused. "Priorities do change. Just keep that firmly in mind, for everyone's sake."

She closed the door, as if putting a period at the end of her proclamation.

As if drawing a more pronounced line so he would be fully aware of it the next time he saw Holly.

"So what exactly are you looking for?" the kind, soft-voiced matron from the bridal store near town square asked Holly.

At the question, Holly held back a sad smile, knowing that Grace, the clerk, was asking about a dress, nothing more. But if Holly were to answer, she might've said something about her baby and a house with a nice little lawn for her child to play on in a quiet neighborhood where ice cream trucks still drove slowly by.

That's all Holly was looking for.

But, instead of voicing that, she pulled out a file of magazine clippings from her big suede purse. The pictures she'd collected back when she and Alan had dated.

So much for wishful thinking.

"Here are some ideas," she said as Grace perused the images.

"We can certainly work with this."

Grace laid the file on the glass table, between the flower-patterned sofas where she and Holly were chatting. She'd offered Holly champagne but had apologized after remembering the pregnancy announcement. So it was club soda all the way.

The shopkeeper stood. "We've got all kinds of choices for Bo Clifton's bride."

Initially, Holly had taken Grace Farthingworth as a conservative who might pass judgment on her and Bo because of the pregnancy—a Swinton supporter. But the older woman hadn't shown even a speck of high-minded derision.

She supposed the woman was more enthusiastic about having Thunder Canyon's potential new first lady as a customer.

"We'll be going with a Wild West theme, if that helps," Holly said.

"So…Annie Oakley? That sort of feel?"

Holly laughed. "No. I'm actually thinking of something in an empire style, if you have that on hand." She touched her tummy.

"Of course." Grace skittered off to the back of the shop, moving fast for a woman with a slight blue tint to her hair and limbs like those of a frail cricket's.

She was back in five minutes to escort Holly to a dressing room with three gowns hanging beside it.

Revealing her first choice, Grace presented a high-waisted taffeta sheath that would've done nicely, but there was another dress that caught Holly's eye.

"This," she said, touching the plastic wrapping.

"The Elizabeth Bennet special?" Grace plucked it out from the other dresses and parted the plastic, showing off the white velvet, the long sleeves, the blue sash. "That's what I like to call it. *Pride and Prejudice* is one of my favorites. With your hair up and curls framing your face under the veil, you'd pull this off wonderfully."

It wasn't the Wild West, but the gown had already captured Holly's heart.

But would Bo like it?

Grace led Holly into the dressing room and pulled the curtain to assure privacy. "I'll be right back with a veil as well as the wrap that goes with the gown."

By the time she returned, Holly was in her dress, flushed as she stared at the vision in the mirror.

A bride looked back out at her—a glowing woman in white velvet, which whispered in a graceful line to the ground. A woman who could've been an angel if she hadn't fallen from her former heights.

When she exited the room, Grace's eyes got misty.

"This is why I love my job," she said, clasping the veil in her hands as if it were a bouquet. She came over and worked the pearled headpiece—all pearls and soft gleam—into Holly's hair.

Then the shopkeeper darted out of the room again and returned with an actual bouquet—white silk flowers—for Holly to hold.

Grace brought her over to a connected set of three long, antique mirrors, and Holly bit her bottom lip as she glanced at every angle. It was as if she was peeking into a fortune-teller's vision. Or, at least, an alternate version of what she could have been.

Because this didn't seem as if it was really happening.

The chimes sounded from the front door of the shop, but before Grace could get there, Holly saw someone else in the mirror behind her.

Bo.

He was taking off his hat, holding it over his heart, as if in awe. In her wildest dreams, she'd only imagined seeing a man react this way to her—like a groom who couldn't take his eyes off of his intended as she walked down the aisle toward him, the rest of their lives before them.

Holly went fluid under his appreciative gaze, even as she told herself that this was all just part of the act, that he had to be this way in front of the shopkeeper.

But Grace wasn't so much paying attention to that as to tradition.

"Bo Clifton? Git. Shoo!"

He came out of whatever acting moment he was experiencing, tossing his hat to the nearest chair. Holly almost wondered if she'd conjured up the entire few seconds.

"Morning, Grace," he said. "I see my bride's in fine hands."

"You're causing bad luck!" Grace was pulling at his coat now.

"It's okay," Holly said. Their marriage would be over before they needed much luck, anyway. "As you might've heard, Bo's a progressive, so he believes in building on tradition rather than rigidly subscribing to it."

The old woman had given up on trying to drag him out. "There're just some things you don't mess with, and seeing your future wife like this is one of them."

"No problem," he said. "We'll make sure to counter

the bad luck by getting Holly something old, something new, something…" He frowned. "What's the rest of it?"

Holly helped him out. "Something borrowed, something blue."

Bo had sauntered closer to her, and she shivered, anticipating the scent and proximity of him.

"You can actually see a bump under the fabric," he said, meaning her belly.

It was true. Her baby curve was slightly more pronounced now that she wasn't wearing baggy sweaters and skirts.

"That's why I like this particular gown," she said. "We'll know Hopper's there, and if I pop by the time the wedding comes, this dress can accommodate the growth."

"Pop?" he asked.

"If I start to grow and resemble a weather balloon."

Grace huffed out another you-shouldn't-be-here sigh in the background as Bo sidled next to Holly, his gaze on her belly, his hand reaching out to it, just as he'd done last evening in the park.

But this time, it seemed that he thought better of touching her bump for some reason, and he pulled his hand back.

A bolt of sorrow hit Holly right in the heart. Had he started thinking of what she would look like when she popped and really began to swell up?

Or was this charade getting to be too much for even him?

He took a painful step away from her and said to Grace, "You're coming to the wedding, right?"

At his change, Holly tried to smile at the shopkeeper in the mirror as her heart crumbled. But why?

Why should it matter?

"I'm invited?" Grace asked.

"Definitely," he said. "Next weekend. We'll send word of the specifics."

"Quick wedding," Grace said. "But I read in the paper just why it'd have to be quick."

Right. All the stories about Holly wanting to wait, then changing her mind as her pregnancy became more obvious…

"The wedding may be fast in the getting here," Bo said, "but I've been in love with Holly for a long time."

Although Holly was getting used to reacting automatically to comments like that, when she smiled at her beloved fiancé, it wasn't as easy as usual.

But Grace wouldn't realize it.

Appeased, the shopkeeper became a Bo fan once again. "Champagne for the groom? Or club soda, as your bride asked for?"

"The soda is good."

And Grace was off once more.

Bo faced Holly in the mirror. He must've seen the questions in her gaze, because he stiffened, as if he wouldn't know how to answer even if she asked him why he'd decided not to touch her.

Six months, Holly thought. Was their short marriage going to be this complicated during that entire time?

"So," he said, brightening up. "Have you mulled over the something old, new, borrowed and blue stuff?"

"I thought you weren't a traditional guy."

"Not true. There're some things I believe in. You know how I feel about my family, for instance."

Yes, she did, and she believed in Bo Clifton one hundred percent when it came to that.

She held up her hand, where their engagement ring sparkled under the shop lights. "Here's something old."

"What about something new?" he asked.

She hugged her belly, indicating the baby while grinning, trying to get out of the funk she'd found herself in.

"I like that. Hopper," he said, and it looked like he wanted to touch the baby's home again.

But he didn't.

Holly tried not to let disappointment nail her. "Something borrowed?"

She thought about how he was sort of borrowing her.

He shrugged. "We'll have to muse about that one."

"Okay. Then that leaves something blue."

"You got that covered."

He stared into her eyes, telling her that he was talking about the color of them.

She almost forgot how to breathe.

Blue, the gorgeous color of his eyes, too.

Then Grace entered the room with the club soda, and Bo disconnected from Holly, as if he'd been discovered doing something he shouldn't.

But it was a good idea for him to realize the difference between the ruse and the reality, wasn't it?

Thank God one of them had it firmly in mind.

Chapter Six

That evening, Bo waited for his dinner guests in his ranch house, which sat on his property near Grant and Steph's spread, Clifton's Pride. His two-story cabin overlooked the creek and, on many nights, he spent the sunset hours on his wraparound porch, listening to the wind, hearing the trickle of water and the croaking of frogs. Farther on down his two hundred acres, his hired hands bunked down in cabins, nearer to the cattle.

But it was getting too cold for porch sitting. And Bo didn't have the patience for it tonight anyway, opting to work in his kitchen instead, getting together the fixings for grilled steaks and salad. Holly had offered to prepare some appetizers and dessert before she came over to his place, too, so he'd accepted, wondering why she hadn't told him she would cook in this kitchen when he'd offered the run of it.

Yet he was trying not to think about Holly right now. Trying not to think about the emotions he'd almost lost hold of at the bridal shop this afternoon.

It'd been a real shock to see her in that dress. A velvet princess. A woman to have and to hold.

But, for all intents and purposes, she wasn't really his. Neither was the baby. So, no matter how much he'd wanted to be a part of that moment, with her staring at herself in the mirror as if seeing a fantasy come true, he'd talked himself out of it, and just in time, too.

Still, he couldn't forget Holly's face when he'd drawn back from touching her on the stomach, where Hopper slept.

Had he let her down in some way today?

A knock sounded on his front door, and he walked over the floor planks to answer it. When he opened up, he found Holly, dressed in her usual wool coat, a roomy plaid skirt, boots and a dark sweater, which seemed to be tighter than the usual variety. He could even see a hint of baby bump under the knit fabric.

A tide of heat rose up in him, a flood that threatened to take him over.

"Come on in," he said, stepping aside, pretending everything was on an even keel.

Her cheeks were rosy from cold. She clutched a couple of shopping bags in her gloved hands, loaded down with the food she'd promised.

"You just could've prepared all that here," he said, repeating himself.

"I already know my way around the other kitchen, so it seemed more efficient to do it at home."

Home.

This wasn't her home, he reminded himself, so why did the word tweak him?

She smiled, a polite stranger after today in the bridal shop. Had she cooked in her own kitchen to show him that she was maintaining a safe remoteness? And just what did her sweet yet distant smile mean now?

Behind her, Bo could see Grant and Steph pull into the drive. He raised his hand in greeting, closing the door partway to keep out the cold as he took the shopping bags from Holly and helped her out of her coat.

Soon, the second half of their party eased open the door, greeting Bo and Holly with hearty how-do-you-dos. Grant was Bo's age, and the cousins also shared the same piercing blue eyes. But Grant had dirty blond hair and was particularly tall—about a half-head higher, even after he took off his cowboy hat and hung it on the rack. He towered over his wife, Steph, a natural blond beauty who was nearly six months pregnant, with the same luminous skin as Holly, her green eyes sparkling with the happiness she and Grant had found together.

They all went to the kitchen, where Steph took the plastic wrapping off of a cheese and fruit plate. Holly uncovered her own dishes: appetizers that included barbecued meatballs and bacon-wrapped water chestnuts, plus a panful of sinfully thick, moist brownies. She'd also brought some nonalcoholic cider for the pregnant girls.

Bo had purchased some cider, too. Had Holly believed that he, the host, had forgotten about her needs?

Or was she just that cussed independent?

As the men grabbed beers from the fridge, the women fell into a conversation about their pregnancies. Under Steph's cable knit sweater and maternity jeans, her tummy was much bigger and rounder than Holly's, but Bo's fiancée seemed comfortable with how she hadn't "popped" yet. He expected most women would be discomfited by looking different from what a lot of people expected at seven months, but not Holly.

Bo poured the cider for the ladies, then joined Grant in the living room, with its river stone fireplace, wooden arrowhead light fixtures and moose antlers above the mantel. It was a real bachelor's den. He wondered if Holly would be getting rid of some of his kitchy belongings when she moved in.

Little did she know that he would go to the mat with her over those light fixtures.

He and Grant leaned back against a leather sofa, watching the women through the peek-a-boo window of his big kitchen.

In spite of what he'd thought before, Holly *did* seem at home in there. He could picture her, as his wife, making herself comfortable in every room.

But what about with Bo? Sometimes it felt as if there was a room inside of him, too, a space that had stood empty for a long time…

Grant said, "It won't be long before Holly's cooking up a lot of meals in there. When's she moving in?"

When Bo had asked his cousin to be his best man, he'd also told him the truth about the marriage. They'd always shared a bond because of the murder in the family, and Bo didn't trust anyone more. That meant Steph was aware of it, too, but no one else besides the Cliftons and Rose knew about the charade. The fewer people who were privy to Bo's private matters, the better.

"We'll be hauling Holly's stuff here after the wedding."

Grant shook his head. "I still can't believe it. You, married. But it stands to reason that you'd be going about it in your own way. With the speed of this wedding, you might as well have just eloped."

"The wedding won't be anything fancy. Nothing more than a party with some I dos involved."

Grant didn't say anything, just took a swig of his beer. It didn't merit a rocket scientist to know that he didn't approve of Bo's scheming.

After he'd swallowed, he said, "Your mom and dad. Are they coming to the ceremony?"

Bo had contacted his parents at their separate homes—one in Billings, the other out of state in Idaho, where his father was enjoying retirement after handing the Thunder Canyon ranch off to Bo. Both had been equally stunned at his announcement.

"My mom got after me for the short notice," Bo said. "She'd already planned a big, nonrefundable trip to Italy that she's been saving up a long time for. She's wanted to go there forever, so I couldn't argue with her about cancelling."

"But you're getting *married,* Bo." Then Grant seemed to remember that it was hardly a marriage.

Bo steeled himself. "She said she'd make it up to me, but I have the feeling Mom would've come if my dad wasn't going to attend."

"She's still up to that? Making you choose between the two of them and considering it a betrayal if you refuse to play that game?"

"I'm afraid so."

He'd tried to say it without sounding affected, but disappointment leaked through, anyway.

Grant noticed. "You watch—they'll both show. Your

mom wouldn't dare miss her son's big day, even if she has no idea it's..." He stopped short of saying "fake."

Bo shrugged. Even his mom and her impossible standards for his father wouldn't ruin this wedding *or* his plans. "You'd think, over the last few years after their divorce, she would've come to terms with all their arguments and differences."

"Aunt Nell could always hold a hell of a grudge. But she'll come around, Bo."

"I'm not sure she will."

Bo jerked his chin toward the kitchen, relaying that he was going to check in with Holly and Steph. It was a good enough excuse to get away from the present discussion.

He scooped up the dishes that the women had been hovering over while they'd laughed and compared more pregnancy notes.

"What do you say we have a seat?" he asked.

Steph walked ahead of him as Holly brought out the rest of the appetizers.

"Sitting sounds just fine to me," Steph said.

Grant chuckled as he waited for her to come around to the front of the sofa, then took the spot next to her. "This coming from a woman who still can't slow down."

"Hey, I've eased off giving the horseback riding lessons for now. I'm pretty good at resting like I should."

"You're pretty good at anything you put a mind to."

He leaned over to kiss her, and they smiled, their lips lingering against each other's for an extra second.

Bo tried not to glance at Holly, even though he probably should be kissing on her, too, being lovebirds just like Grant and Steph.

But he kept recalling his talk with Rose.

He wouldn't cross a line.

Not unless Holly gave him a sign.

The realization jarred him, and he lost the battle to keep his gaze off of her. She'd taken a seat in the cushioned leather chair opposite his. They were across the big oaken table from each other, but it didn't seem like much space at all when she met his gaze, too.

It felt as if the room got smaller, bringing him toward her, pushing them together…

Holly was the first to glance away, her forehead creased.

Something dropped within Bo. But what was it?

What was happening with them?

She filled a plate with appetizers. "Grant, you've done such a great job with the resort. It looks fantastic. I can see why it's got such a reputation."

"I'm doing my best," he said as Holly handed him the plate, the consummate hostess. She probably would've prepared something for Steph, too, but their other guest had already piled her plate high, grinning at Grant as he raised an eyebrow to her.

Bo said, "Things will turn around for the resort."

"Is that the politician speaking or just a hopeful citizen of Thunder Canyon?" Grant asked.

"They're one and the same." He leaned his forearms on his thighs, his beer dangling from his fingers. "You guys ever hear the story about the farmer in old Rome who was called away from his fields to fulfill his civic duty as a senator? He answered the call, but he didn't do it because he wanted personal power or money. He did it because it was right. Because his fellow folk needed someone to speak up for them. And after his time on duty, he went back to his farm and took up his fields again." Bo nodded. "That's the kind of politician I'd like to be—the kind they all should be. That's a hero."

Holly was watching him with a light in her eyes. It might've been admiration, and it spread to him, swirling inside his chest.

What would it be like to wake up every morning, seeing this expression on someone's face?

On *Holly's* face?

Steph was looking at the both of them, as if she'd seen what had passed in their gazes.

Holly snapped the moment when she softly asked, "What makes you answer this certain call of duty, Bo? Why did you want to step up and run for mayor?"

Grant lowered his head. He already knew. So did Steph.

Before now, Bo hadn't told Holly much about himself. There'd been no need, but the words wouldn't sit still in him as the passion—the anger—reared up again, just as it did every once in a while, a reminder of what shouldn't be tolerated in this world.

"You remember what happened at the Callister Breaks," he said to Holly.

She nodded, pressing her lips together, as if she regretted bringing it up. But it was too late now.

Bo continued. "Rustlers took the lives of my uncle John and Andre Julen, and there's not a day that goes by when I don't remember. And I can't even imagine how Grant and Steph must feel about it."

They'd discovered the bodies—Grant, who'd just gotten out of college, and Steph, who'd been a mere teenager. No child should've ever seen their dad like that, bloodied, tied up…

Bo gripped his beer bottle as Holly turned to Grant and Steph.

"I'm so sorry."

She was apologizing for the deaths *and* encouraging the topic, even though she clearly hadn't known what she was doing by asking Bo about his reasons for campaigning.

Grant leaned back against the sofa, Steph in the crook of his arm. "It's taken years, but we've come to peace with it."

"But there's no forgetting it," Bo said. "Because, after that day, the world changed. The cracks in it became more obvious. It took me a long time to figure out how to fill those fissures though. Then I saw people like Grant making Thunder Canyon a better place through the resort, helping this town to prosper and highlighting the best things about it. I saw Steph—absolutely in love with this place and willing to do anything for it. And you, Holly—there were people like you who came out of their homes and tried to uplift the community through their actions. I could do the same, I realized. I could make a difference."

He could change things.

And what about Bo Clifton? an unwelcome voice from the dark of his head asked. *Aren't there some changes the ultimate bachelor could make in himself, along with the ones he's advocating for Thunder Canyon?*

Grant delicately veered away from the subject by lifting his beer and saying, "To a better, brighter Thunder Canyon."

All of them picked up their drinks and toasted, yet Bo

couldn't help but notice that Holly was pretty quiet for the rest of the night, as if he'd said too damned much.

As if she'd gotten in way too deep, just as he feared he had.

The following week dashed by, and there was nothing Holly could do to stop it.

It was full of wedding gown fittings, plus making sure her bridesmaids knew that they only had to wear a light blue dress and weren't expected to be fabric-coordinated. It was crammed with meetings with Rose and Trisha, the retired wedding coordinator, to see that everything was on track.

And on the actual day of the wedding, Holly took a deep breath, going forward with all of it, even if there'd been a whole lot of misgivings eating away at her since the dinner with Grant and Steph.

Now, as she sat in a guest bedroom in Bo's house, she pinned up the last of her curls, then adjusted her bridal veil's headdress. In the mirror, the room expanded around her, surreal, a strange dream she couldn't wake up from.

This would be her room when she officially moved in with Bo, although she hadn't transferred her personal items here yet.

Her own bedroom, just down the hall from his.

Erika came up behind her, putting her hands on Holly's shoulders. The matron of honor was garbed in a light blue velvet dress that Bo had insisted on purchasing.

Outside, Holly could hear music—the country band that been hired. They were playing a Western-tinged

"Can I Have This Dance," a love song that'd been popular even before she was born.

Erika spoke. "Something's been bothering you ever since last weekend."

Holly hadn't told her friend about the dinner yet, but now the room, with its white walls and simple mountain landscape paintings, had the air of a confessional.

A last-chance way station on this crazy ride.

"I never expected to think of Bo as more than a…" Holly didn't know how to put it.

Erika waited her out.

"…a *guy*." No, that wasn't good enough. "What I mean is that Bo was *Bo*—the man everybody thinks is so great. The superficial smiling person you see around town on those posters. We didn't talk about anything deep. I didn't even tell him much about Alan, but then… last weekend…"

"Ah," Erika said. "Something broke open."

"I saw a whole new side to him."

And she hadn't known what to do afterward, as the conversation between her and Bo and their guests had lightened up significantly over the rest of the appetizers, then dinner. It was as if the talk of the murders—and their effect on Bo and the rest of the Cliftons—hadn't occurred at all.

During the week, every time Holly had gone to his campaign office, or every time he would walk her through town to greet the citizens and show off her blossoming belly, she'd felt caught in a sort of limbo. Once, a few days ago, as they'd lunched at the Hitching Post, she'd tried to broach the subject of the dinner, but Bo had expertly steered her off course with one of his lighthearted grins.

"Don't you worry about a thing," he said, as if it was a touchstone for him.

But why should she care about any of it when she and her baby would be out of here soon, anyway?

"I'd convinced myself that Bo wasn't all that complex," Holly added, "but that isn't necessarily true."

"It was easier when he was just a charmer, huh?"

"Much." Holly traced a bottle of honey-scented perfume she'd brought with her. The scent turned her stomach now. "I never really thought about how much Bo and his family have gone through. In comparison to him, I haven't experienced anything."

Perhaps Arthur Swinton was right every time he insinuated in the press that Bo was predatory for going after a woman thirteen years his junior. "Maybe this really was a bad idea."

Or maybe Holly was merely afraid that she'd underestimated so much about Bo.

Including her feelings for him…

Erika squeezed Holly's shoulders. "As you know, I never did understand why you'd choose a fake marriage over single motherhood. This might only be the start of your problems, Holly."

No argument there. But was this easier than it would've been to just tell the truth to her family? To try and make it on her own with her child?

Holly felt her baby moving in her, and in a moment of whimsy, she could almost imagine that the baby already was looking around for Bo. She actually had the gut feeling that her child rather liked Bo, even though Holly knew she might only be justifying the choices she'd made.

Then again, there'd been times with Bo when she'd

truly been content. Actually, scratch that. She'd been *happy.* Like when they'd sat on that park bench and he'd put his hand on her tummy and she'd thought, *What if…?*

The band from outside started playing Pachelbel's "Canon in D." It was Holly's cue.

She'd given him her word.

She was going to do this, for her baby.

For…

Not knowing how to complete that thought, Holly got up from the chair, holding her bouquet of wildflowers in one hand, palming the bottom of her belly in the other. During the last week, there'd been a noticeable curving of her tummy—finally—and the roundness of her baby showed clearly under her dress.

"You're really doing this," Erika said.

"I made a promise."

And that was the most important thing, right? That's why she was going to carry on…

Erika kept any other objections to herself as she and Holly came out and into the hallway. Then, in the next wonderland minute, Holly was outside, where the clouds had revealed a warming sun and the Wild West theme was in full play. Her dad was waiting for her by the wildflower-lined aisle, which arrowed between the hay bales that served as seats.

She saw a small group of her college pals sitting together, smiling in spite of their surprise at Holly's lightning-quick wedding news and her pregnancy.

It also seemed as if most of Thunder Canyon had turned up. Vaguely, Holly recognized Dillon Traub, who seemed to be thinking of his own upcoming wedding to Erika as he held little Emilia and watched Holly's matron of honor, his heart in his eyes. Near him, his cousins Dax and DJ sat with their wives and kids. Marlon Cates and Haley Anderson, Holly's ROOTS coordinator, were also here for the nuptials. Marlon's twin, Matt, sat on the other side of him, a more serious version of the brother who always seemed to have a twinkle in his eyes.

Holly's gaze traveled forward to where Grant was standing up for the groom, even though Holly knew he was doing it against his better judgment.

Then she got to Bo.

Her body flared with a desire that burned as she saw the same look on his face that he'd worn in the bridal shop when he'd first spied her in this gown.

Grant nudged his cousin, but Bo's expression didn't change; he kept wearing it right along with that ever-present Stetson. She'd half expected him to, even now, be wearing the rest of his cowboy gear, yet, instead, he had on a black tuxedo that put all the other men who'd ever worn one to shame.

A cowboy gentleman.

Hers.

And it didn't even seem like a lie right now—her wanting to get down the aisle as quickly as possible, her wanting to just be near enough to him so that she could feel the tingle of his presence nearby.

As "The Wedding March" kicked in, Holly went to her father and took the first step toward Bo.

Then another.

Then it was as if she'd lost time, all the minutes tumbling away to the moment when she heard, "You may now kiss the bride."

Bo turned to her, carefully lifting her veil, folding it back over her head.

Holly's pulse was going so fast that it threatened to spin right out of her, and as Bo got that grin on his face—*Don't worry about a thing*—he lowered his mouth to hers.

Closing her eyes, Holly felt his lips pressing, warm, soft, a world away from any kiss she'd ever felt before.

Wrapping an arm around his neck, she pressed right back, desire welling in her as she tasted Bo—a tinge of mint, a hint of an alternate future she might've had if things had been different and she really *had* met Bo in Bozeman…

She leaned back, and Bo took advantage, taking her all the way into his arms and performing a *Gone with the Wind* embrace that pleased the crowd to no end.

They cheered as Holly came up for air, Bo's lips still right above hers, so close that her mouth still vibrated.

He smiled down at her, his gaze a little wild, just like the Bo she'd heard rumors about before. The untamed bachelor.

He also looked like a man who wanted much more than a kiss.

When he brought her back to a stand, Holly had to claim her balance, and her hand flew to her headdress, as if it would help her to steady herself.

Her lips still tingled, her chest light, as if he'd stolen more than the breath from her.

As she looked out at her friends and family, they looked back, clapping loudly. They saw her as a true bride, didn't they?

For now, Holly actually felt like one, and she clung to the sensation, knowing that all too soon she would have to let it go.

After the ceremony and the pictures with the professional photographer that followed, Holly excused herself to go to the house and freshen up.

And damned if Bo wasn't still under the enchantment of that kiss at the altar.

As he waited in the living room, he could hear the band strike up the first tune on their reception song list—the lively "Orange Blossom Special." His heart, which had never really recovered from that kiss, either, beat in stomping time to the music, racing.

That kiss... It had rocked him when he hadn't been expecting anything of the sort to happen. It had simultaneously been soft and earth-shattering, and Bo had no idea how that could even be possible.

Get ahold of yourself, he thought as he sat on the edge of the sofa, tapping his fingers on his thigh, out of time to the music. *Remember what Holly is to you.*

And then she came out of the hallway.

It was almost as if she was walking down the aisle all over again, and he felt the same jump-start of his pulse, the same abrasions that scratched fire through his core.

She'd taken off her veil, leaving a few stray curls to tickle her neck. But she was still carrying that wildflower bouquet, though she was losing petals by the moment.

When he'd caught his breath sufficiently enough to speak, he raised a finger. "Just one more thing before we go back out there."

He reached next to him on the sofa, grabbing an old Shady Brady cowboy hat that used to belong to his grandmother during her honky-tonk days. The relaxed straw gave it a lethargic shape, but the band of fluffy brown, white and black feathers lent it a lot of spirit.

"Something borrowed," he said, going to Holly and fixing it on her head.

Some women would've complained about what their hair might look like after taking off the hat, but not his bride.

"I love it!" she said, laughing.

"This belonged to Grandma, too."

Holly bit her bottom lip, her gaze catching Bo's, and his gut clenched.

"We've got a lot to thank her for, don't we?" she asked. "First the ring, now..."

"If she was here, she'd definitely be asking for that hat back after you get your fill of it." He'd reverted to small talk as quickly as possible. No more emotional stuff. He'd left that behind last weekend, knowing he couldn't handle anything beyond what he'd already revealed to her.

He held out his arm, and she linked hers in his.

"Shall we?" he asked.

She nodded, and all seemed back to rights—a bride and a groom made to order for a political plan.

They stepped out of the back door of his house to a blast of fiddles and guitars from the band, which was playing from the back of a long flatbed truck stacked with hay bales and decorated with bandanas and gingham. Smoke from the barbecue traced the air, along with shouts of joy from the crowd. To the right, the creek burbled merrily, and several couples stood by it, drinks in hand to toast the emerging newlyweds. To the left, kids ran around playing the games Trish the coordinator had thought up to amuse them: horseshoes, straw horse lassoing, a treasure hunt.

It wasn't long until Bo was separated from Holly while they welcomed their guests, most of whom obviously didn't see the wedding for what it really had been.

He snuck a look at Holly, missing her again for some reason, although she wasn't but five feet away. Maybe the guests had seen all those looks he'd been secretly casting at her. Was that why things had gone so smoothly, because the attendees believed those glances?

When he caught her subtly peeking over at him, too, his heart twisted up, just as addled as his brain was.

Grant was the first one who made it over to them, along with Steph, and they did a fine job of not giving Bo their don't-blow-it expressions as they moved on to Holly.

Connor McFarlane and his fiancée, Tori Jones, followed. Then came Dillon Traub, Erika's fiancé, who vigorously shook Bo's hand.

"Congratulations," he said.

"The same will be in order for you, come next month," Bo said. "You nervous, doc?"

"Not on your life." The man's dark blond hair caught glints from a sun that'd been kind enough to make an appearance today. "Besides marrying the woman of my dreams, my family's coming to town. My brother, Corey, and the other Texas Traubs. Thunder Canyon won't know what to do with us."

And then it was on to the others, including Holly's brothers, who grudgingly shook Bo's hand in turn.

"You'd better take care of her," Hollis said.

Dean, more of the silent type, nodded, although Bo knew he meant the warning just as much as Hollis did. Nick only looked Bo up and down before shaking his hand, too, then going to his sister, who got a big hug.

Progress.

Hell, Hank Pritchett even gave Bo a most father-in-law-like embrace when it came to his turn.

After what seemed to be about a hundred handshakes, the most important man in Bo's life finally showed.

When Bo saw his father, with his craggy skin, gray hair and the charcoal suit he'd been wearing every Sunday to church for decades, he pulled him in for the most crushing hug of all. He'd met with his dad just before the ceremony, but he was just as glad to greet his father now as he'd been then.

"Hey, now!" Carlton Clifton said. "Did you expect me to take off before the cake was served?"

"No. You wouldn't leave me to face all this alone."

The comment betrayed Bo's biggest letdown—that his mom hadn't shown up. See what a busted marriage got you? Disappointment. Fortunately, he was already prepared for his own marriage to end.

She'd stuck to her guns about not attending if Carlton was going to be there. She'd expected Bo to pick between her and her ex-husband, and she was punishing her son for failing in his decision.

But he would live. He'd been coping for years now.

Bo leaned over to Holly and laid his hand on her arm. She turned to him, seemingly breathless. Erika, who she'd been talking to, walked away, keeping a friendly yet cautious eye on Bo.

But he was too caught in the moment to dwell on it. "Holly, you remember my dad?"

"Yes." Her smile was wide, excited. "Thank you so much for being here, Mr. Clifton."

His father embraced Holly with all the bliss of a dad who'd never thought to see a daughter-in-law in the family, especially one as wonderful as her.

Bo felt gouged. *He* was going to end up disappointing his father when the marriage eventually "fell apart."

Unless…

Unless what? There was no "unless." Changing Thunder Canyon was one thing, but changing his own stripes and allowing someone in his heart, just as his dad had done?

Wasn't going to happen. Bo wasn't ever going to allow himself to be as crushed as his father.

His dad held Holly at arm's length. "Welcome to the family."

Too bad his mom wasn't here to say the same.

Even as Bo thought it, Holly glanced at him, and he knew that she sensed that something was wrong.

The sadness had to be written all over him.

Bucking up, Bo grinned, putting an arm around her and his father, pretending as if this family union was going to last.

And even wishing in his heart of hearts that it was possible.

Chapter Seven

An exclusive honeymoon suite in the resort's main lodge had been booked for them. But after Holly and Bo were cheered out of the wedding reception with a shower of wildflowers tossed by their guests, Holly was ready to crash on anything—even an air mattress in the back of a pickup.

Yet she was the mayor candidate's wife now, and Bo had seen to it that she would be treated like one.

As she entered their room ahead of Bo and the bellboy, her nerves reared up, bucking and pawing.

It wasn't due to the extraordinary sunset view of the private cottages and mountains outside of a window that stretched from one end of the suite to the other. Her anxiety hadn't even been spurred by the luxuries, such as a wide-screen plasma TV, a minibar and a linen-draped dining table that had been set up in the connected lounge, complete with silver candlesticks and scattered rose petals…

As Holly rested her luggage on the thick carpet, she tried not to glance again into the *other* room through the adjoining door, where a king-size bed peeked through sheer drapes of *A Thousand and One Nights* netting. A hot tub big enough for two waited nearby.

What had she gotten herself into?

Bo folded a tip into the bellboy's palm, and the kid thanked him, leaving with a huge smile on his face, closing the door behind him.

The slight click of the lock jerked Holly's next to last nerve.

"So…?" Bo asked, sauntering to the lounge area, tossing his overnight bag onto a cushiony velvet sofa. "What do you think?"

How could he be so calm? Weren't the rose petals, the hot tub—or good heavens, *the bed?*—freaking him out in the least?

No, of course not. Bo, still dressed in his tuxedo and cowboy hat, was taking all the accoutrements of their charade in stride. In fact, he had that devilish gleam in his eyes again, as if he'd been waiting to see her reaction to what he must've known would be waiting for them inside this room.

Okay. She could be casual about this, as well. After all, the hotel staff *needed* to believe things were going to get romantic on this well-publicized wedding night, so there would have to be an ooo-la-la dinner and so on.

She could play along, just like always.

Holly went to the window. If she was going to comment on anything, it was going to be the view. "The coordinator really did her job right. I'll have to tell Rose that this room was a good call."

"Only the best for my bride." Bo fell back onto the sofa, kicking his booted feet up on the wide mahogany table and tossing his hat onto a nearby chair. Clasping his hands behind his head, he reclined, sending a roguish waggle of his brows to Holly. "What do we do now?"

Za-zoom.

Holly now knew what it sounded like when anxiety shot through the roof and into the stratosphere.

What to say to him, her *husband?*

What to *do* with him…?

Get yourself in order, Hol. "First things first," she said calmly.

He kept a single eyebrow raised, his mouth curved in one of those grins that forever twanged her pulse. "And what comes first with us, darlin'?"

He was teasing her, and the practical, no-nonsense Holly had no problem being blunt.

"How about we flip a coin to see who gets that bed tonight?"

He laughed. "Touché. Just for that, you win the mattress. I'll take the sofa."

Thank goodness it broke the tension, and she laughed a little, too, in spite of how much she meant the comment. It felt good to be able to make light of this ridiculous situation—this surreal bend of a mirror that was somehow reflecting her life right back at her in a way she'd never pictured before.

Bo leaned forward on the sofa, his bright blue eyes brimming with more humor…and maybe even something else that Holly didn't want to dwell on.

A true invitation to start a honeymoon…?

"And here I thought a romantic wedding would knock your boots off," he said. "Just what does it take to win you over?"

A blast of desire roared through her, even though he wasn't—and couldn't be—serious. But before they ventured into uncomfortable territory, Bo grabbed the TV remote and started flipping through the channels, landing on a digital music station.

An old forties tune played, slow and sensual, warmed by the beat of a bass and the sway of clarinets.

Surely Bo wasn't trying to seduce her.

Holly smoothed down the skirt of her wedding gown, not knowing what else to do.

She had to be imagining things. Bo was just being Bo, making the best out of their situation. He was a flirt, but he was even more of a gentleman.

Or so she hoped.

Besides, as far as she'd heard from the grapevine, Bo had a certain type of woman that he gravitated toward, and it didn't include one whose belly was just beginning to stick out from here to there with another man's baby.

Then Holly remembered their wedding kiss—the way his lips had fit against hers, the fact that he'd lingered, his mouth just a breath away, as if he'd wanted the moment to last and last…

A knock sounded on the door, and Holly just about jumped out of her skin.

Bo stood from the sofa and went to get it. "Dinner is served."

"I'm not really that…"

"You've got to be hungry. I didn't see you eat a thing at the reception."

He'd been watching?

Her stomach gurgled. Darn Bo, but he was right. Still, wouldn't it be the worst idea ever to sit at that table with him, basking in the candlelight and mood music, taking their so-called honeymoon even a millimeter farther than it should go?

"My dress," she said, gesturing to the wedding gown she hadn't changed out of yet. "I don't want to spill anything on it, so I can just eat later."

By herself. In her separate bed.

"Excuses, excuses," he said, opening the door to the waiter.

As soon as Holly caught the aroma of the food, she lost some of her willpower. She just stood there by the window, watching as the room service employee lit the candles, the wicks flickering with dim, come-hither light. Then he set down an ice bucket of nonalcoholic wine, along with covered dishes he announced as cream of leek and potato soup, salad, Brussels sprouts browned with cheese, French bread and roasted chicken.

Oh, man.

After Bo signed the ticket and the server bowed his way out of the room, Holly ventured to the table. The tempting smells were too much.

"And for the finale…?" Bo said, gesturing to a cart that the waiter had left behind. He opened the lid on the remaining dish, revealing a plate of chocolate-covered strawberries.

Her stomach grumbled again, and she thought she could feel the baby squirming around with agreement.

Holly had to take care of herself and her child,

anyway, so she sat in her chair. Bo pushed it forward, then took her napkin, leaning over to lay it over her lap and gently cover her.

The soft touch of linen over her thighs felt like a vibrating weight, and heat crept up and down, coating her.

Chocolate, candlelight and sexy music.

Her heartbeat felt like it was powered by gusts of light, urging steam.

What if Bo made even stronger overtures? And… well, what if she gave in, just as easily as she'd just done with the food?

No. No way she would. But *if* she did, what would Bo expect out of her? A lot of experienced moves, like the women he no doubt usually dated?

What if he found Holly lacking in experience compared to them? She had been with one guy her entire life, and Bo…

Just how *many* women had he made love to during his thirty-five years?

"Relax, Holly." Bo's voice was low enough to coast over her skin as he sat in the chair opposite her. Somehow, he could read her. Maybe he didn't know every thought tearing through her head, but this man was intuitive, especially when it came to her, it seemed.

"I am relaxed," Holly said.

Ignoring the obvious, Bo smiled and fixed his napkin over his own lap. "We're not going to do anything you don't want to do tonight."

Was he thinking she wanted to do *something?*

Blood rushed to her face, and it felt as if her cheeks were neon signals, beating out a heated message for him to make bolder moves.

If she didn't lay everything out for him now in no uncertain terms, she might regret it. "I don't know why you'd think that *I'd* be thinking of doing anything with you. We both know where we stand."

He swept a glance over her, and it seemed to last so long that she thought she would start to simmer under it.

But then he nodded, apparently unaffected, still grinning and having a good old time.

"Then there it is," he said.

He took the bottle from the ice bucket and poured some sparkling cider for them both. He toasted her, clinking his glass to hers, then drinking up, not pressing the issue any further.

Not even as the candlelight flickered on, marking the passing moments with beats of burning light.

Holly ate her salad as silence reigned at the table, the music lyrics inserting the wrong words between them—promises of kisses and eternities and love, love, love.

There had to be a way to break this tension. Had to be a way to tell him that he should probably just turn off the music and stop pretending that they were anything but business partners.

She thought about subjects that always brought a night up cold.

Small talk. Other people.

Ex-girlfriends.

Heh.

She shuffled a piece of lettuce around her chilled plate with her fork. "You seem to be an expert in these romantic dinners."

Bo paused, a chunk of roast chicken poised on the

fork above his plate. The arch of his eyebrow told her that he knew exactly what she was up to.

"I've had a few," he said.

"So how long do you think it'll be before you start dating again? I mean, after our annulment?"

She might as well have just sprayed him with a scent named *There Will Be No Nookie Tonight.*

"Holly," he said. "I told you that you can relax. I'm not going to put any kind of pressure on you."

Oh, but if only his eyes were promising the same thing…

They ate a little bit more, but by now, curiosity really was starting to get the better of Holly. She'd asked a question as a diversionary tactic, but he hadn't answered, and she'd been half hoping he would.

She set down her wine glass. "Bo, in all honesty, I really am wondering. For the six months of our marriage, what do you plan to do about…?"

"Sex?"

Ooh. She wished he hadn't gone and said *the word.* But now that it was out there, it couldn't be ignored.

"Half a year is a long time," she said.

"Haven't you ever lasted that long?"

She ignored that. "I mean it, Bo. Simply from a political standpoint, I think you already know that if you decide to go outside of our marriage, whether it's real or not, for…satisfaction…there'll be trouble for you."

He gave her one of those looks that she couldn't file under his usual categories: the flirt, the gentleman, the politician.

It actually reminded her of the night when he'd talked about his reasons for wanting to be mayor….

Then he stuck his fork into a Brussels sprout. "I'll be

too busy to think of anything but my job, Holly. Besides, in the end, after we announce our annulment, I'm sure a lot of the town will be disappointed in me for being unable to make a marriage with you work, so I wouldn't dare compound their ire by being unfaithful to you."

"You're going to be a monk?"

"I plan to devote myself to *them,* heart and soul."

It all should've sounded so cynical, but somehow it didn't, maybe because Holly knew that Bo's heart really was in the right place when it came to Thunder Canyon.

Longing sifted through Holly. What would it be like if someone felt that way about *her?* Willing to risk their reputation, their time, their…everything?

And what if that man had been Bo?

Don't even wonder, she thought. *Don't let all these honeymoon trappings get to you.*

"You've probably figured out that I'm not the marrying type, anyway," he said, picking up his glass to wash down that Brussels sprout.

"Why do you say that?"

When he looked into her eyes, it was with a question that dug deep. Thing was, Holly didn't understand what he was asking until she recalled this afternoon, when he'd seemed so forlorn about his mother not being at the ceremony.

Another piece of Bo's puzzle fell into place, right inside her chest where, bit by bit, he was becoming a more complete part of her.

A part that would no doubt crumble to pieces again right after this marriage was over.

Holly's expression seemed so sad, and Bo couldn't do anything but glance away from her, focusing once again on eating, shoving the food into his mouth, hardly tasting it.

"I'm sorry about your parents," Holly said.

"No need to be."

She hesitated, as if seeing straight through his defenses. Then she said, "All right," and stirred her soup with a spoon.

The seconds ticked by, piling one upon another, adding more weight on him until he couldn't stand it any more.

"You must've heard the details about my parents' divorce." And a person like Holly would've been astute enough to do the math and figure out that one dissatisfied parent plus another equaled a son who saw that relationships were made to fail.

"I heard bits and pieces," she said. "I wish your mom would've forgotten about her disappointments and come to the ceremony for your sake, no matter how much she didn't want to run into your dad."

"She said something about attending my inauguration, if it happens."

"What if your dad's there, too?"

Bo's laugh was short. "It'll be up to me to make sure he doesn't come. You see, in her eyes, he got the wedding, and she'll get a day that's important, too. Fifty-fifty split down the middle, just like a division in property."

"Oh, Bo."

Compassion filled her voice and he absorbed it. But he wrung it out of himself as soon as possible.

This was their honeymoon—or, at least, this was a night that wasn't made for deep talk or deep *anything*. Hell, even if Bo had ordered up the candlelight and seductive music, he knew damned well that he was dancing awfully close to that line he and Rose had talked about. He'd even caught a yearning glint in Holly's gaze a time or two, as if she was recalling their wedding kiss and wondering what it would be like to take it to the honeymoon suite.

So why had he been flirting with that line, making insinuations and setting the stage for a seduction?

Was he seeing if she was open to one?

God, he was playing with fire, and it was as if he couldn't stop himself.

The best thing he could do would be to let Holly continue with this sobering discussion, covering a topic that might just provide an invisible wall between them, a clear sign that he should stay on one side and her on the other.

She still hadn't eaten that soup. "I suppose I understand what you're saying about property. I felt like that with Alan, except he didn't seem all that interested in taking what he left behind, namely a child."

"He didn't know what he was giving up," Bo said without checking himself.

Holly's smile was sorrowful, and it just about cracked Bo's heart in two.

But that was only because he felt for her situation, not because she still might be in love with Alan.

Or that Bo himself might be…

When she continued, he silently thanked her for cutting him off.

"I tell myself every day that him leaving me was for the best," she said. "Can you imagine if I'd gone through with marrying Alan and then, years later, *that's* when he decided that his career was his true love?"

"Would that have hurt less?"

"I'm not sure. It might have been worse. At least by ditching me now, he made sure my child won't remember him."

Her comment made Bo reconsider that she might still be in love with her ex. "You don't have feelings for him anymore?"

Holly paused, then said, "I can't imagine loving someone who has no respect for me or the baby he helped to create. I couldn't love *myself* if I had someone like that in my life, because I was raised to believe that I'm better than that."

Her maturity struck him. He almost even forgot about their age difference until he reminded himself of it again, just as he kept repeating so many reasons that this wasn't a real marriage.

Holly said, "The bottom line is that I didn't have the chance to give Alan all of me—not like how my dad and mom gave themselves to each other." She sighed. "Now, there was a love that went right."

Bo didn't remind her that it had gone right until Holly's mom had passed on. He wasn't about to point out that, even with her parents, there'd been heartbreak, just of another sort.

"Even if your parents had a good marriage," he said, "not everyone has to wed in a traditional sense. Some of us can just enjoy the company of others on this level. As friends. Colleagues."

Holly took that in, as if understanding what he was really saying.

He wasn't capable of more than this kind of marriage.

She smiled, accepting it. "I just might end up

liking life as your colleague, Bo, even just for a few months."

He ignored the tipsy slant of his heart. "I hope I get to be there even afterward for you and Baby. I owe you big, Holly."

"No one owes anyone."

As if they'd come to some kind of truce, they went back to their meals, filling up on the best the resort had to offer.

By the time they'd finished the chocolate-dipped strawberries, Holly was far more relaxed, holding her tummy, rubbing it as if she was comforting herself as well as her child.

Just watching her, Bo longed to be a part of it. Mother and baby. His wife and child.

All it might take was a touch of his fingertips over her cheek. A brush against her neck, her collarbones… lower.

Hotter.

His groin tightened, his body's temperature rising and erasing every bit of common sense from each individual cell.

Except for the ones in his brain.

You want to commit yourself? Because taking her to bed would sure do it with a woman like Holly.

Still, the heat rose, nearly shutting out one last thought.

Being with her is going to change you, and you know it….

Holly stretched in her chair; she'd obviously gotten comfortable with the gentleman Bo had seemed to be during the last part of their dinner—the groom who'd promised not to do anything she didn't want to do.

But that groom was watching the way her wedding dress pushed up the swell of her breasts under the velvet. He was imagining how it would feel to cup his hands over her, sketching over the curves, the budding centers…

She slowly stood. "I'm beat. Would you mind if I got ready to hit the hay?"

"Go ahead," he said.

She moved to the baggage she'd left near the door, then went to the bedroom. Bo rose from his own chair, flames coursing through him, beating, demanding.

She didn't shut the bedroom door behind her, so he could see her walking to the spacious marble bathroom, where she did close herself in.

Bo shut off the TV, then went to the window, looking out at the wide Montana night sky with its glitter of stars winking back at him, as if encouraging every thud of his pulse.

Your wife. Your bride…

When he heard Holly come out of the bathroom, he went to her.

She'd just climbed onto the bed when she saw him come through the door. He glimpsed white cotton, modest and sweet, as she pulled the covers over her chest.

But there was that look in her eyes again.

The wanting.

The needing.

I do, she'd said earlier today at the altar. And he'd said it, too.

I do.

He went to her bedside, and as her eyes widened, he slipped a hand behind her head, leaning over.

She hitched in a breath, just before he pressed his lips to her forehead.

"Night, darlin'," he said, pulling himself away before he destroyed everything.

He only had time to see the shape of her mouth—a half gape of shock, the softness of a pair of lips that had been all too willing to be kissed senseless—as he left the room and headed for the couch.

There, Bo didn't sleep a wink, just like most men on their wedding nights.

Except, for him, it was for a different reason altogether.

The next morning, after they'd stayed out of each other's way, getting ready, eating breakfast, ignoring everything about the night before, Holly and Bo had checked out of the resort, going straight to the Rockin' C.

There, he had moved Holly's scant belongings into his own house while she took care of light unpacking. The plan was to keep out of the public eye over the rest of the weekend during their short honeymoon, and they did it well, sticking to their strategy. They even managed to steer clear of one another for the rest of the day, too, grabbing their own meals until it came time for Holly to climb into her new bed in her new home.

Yes, *her* home now, even though it was going to take some time to get used to it.

When Monday morning arrived, Bo left early for the campaign office, and Holly told herself that this was okay, too. It was part of the plan, just like everything else.

Come noon, after she'd run her own errands, she

went to meet him, braving the public eye once again, the campaign going full speed ahead as they strolled arm and arm down a street lined with a row of small shops, some of which were vacant storefronts. Even so, the Old West feel, with the occasional hitching post and weathered wood walkway, still held its charm, just as Thunder Canyon would always hold its own.

Holly tried not to think about how they were putting on a display for the town, like the Halloween decorations that were beginning to color some of the windows with fake autumn leaves, flying witches, gangly skeletons.

As they passed townsfolk, nodding at them, thanking them for the wedding congratulations and felicitations, Holly asked, “How was work today?”

“The usual,” Bo said, tipping his hat to an older couple who gave him a considering look as they walked on.

He would be trying to win every single vote for the next few weeks, and Holly added her own sparkling smile every time, too.

But it wasn’t easy, holding hands with him like this, pretending. Every one of the passersby knew that there’d been a mini-honeymoon and, earlier, a couple had even wondered when Holly and Bo were going to find time for a longer trip, if Bo should win the election.

“Being with Bo now is honeymoon enough,” Holly said, taking it upon herself to answer.

But little did the townsfolk know that there really *had* almost been a honeymoon for Holly on her wedding night, when Bo had appeared at her bedside.

And she’d been ready for him, God help her. After he’d kissed her on the forehead, she’d nearly forgotten that it would be a terrible notion to pull him down to her for a longer, deeper kiss, and then some.

He'd slept on the sofa the whole night while she'd tangled herself up in her sheets, wondering if—no, hoping that—he would open up her bedroom door and slip into bed with her. She'd ached and ached for it, although she'd been too afraid to go to him.

It would've ruined their plans. Would've messed her up good, too, because she couldn't afford another repeat of Alan, where her heart was torn ragged....

She almost missed a step on the planked walkway, and Bo scooped his arm around her, holding her up.

"Whoops," she said.

While he kept touching Holly, he watched her with that curious look, as if he didn't understand what was going on between them any more than she did.

"Holly..." he said.

Then a flashbulb interrupted the moment.

Again.

Holly was getting used to blinking after pictures, but unlike the last time she and Bo had been unprepared during a candid moment, he went to shake this photographer's hand.

No, unlike the night in the park, when they'd been flashbulb-attacked while Bo had touched her belly, her husband actually welcomed a reporter from a lifestyles magazine based outside of Thunder Canyon. The publication had a pretty decent circulation within the state, and they'd become interested in Bo's maverick campaign.

The woman, a spritely forty-something, said, "I thought I'd get a head start on our interview. I know it's a few hours away, but I couldn't resist that shot of you two. Those are the kind of pictures that won over people to the likes of Princess Di and Prince Charles. Remember when they were in their early stages of courtship? You remind me of them."

The comparison withered within Holly. Di and Charles' romance had turned out to be a manufactured facade, with the princess's unrequited love for her prince. Charles's heart had belonged to another woman, and Diana never had a shot, living a sorrowful life.

Their fairy tale had been a lie.

As they said good-bye to the reporter, Holly tried not to walk with a tension-filled gait that would only show how *these* lies were tying her up.

When she and Bo came to a tiny baby boutique, a newer business that seemed to be floundering based on the constant Sale! sign in its window, Bo opened up the door for her, his hand on her back as he ushered her in.

He was no doubt aware that their reporter had been trailing them from a near distance. Now, Holly could see her outside the window, discreetly keeping tabs on her subjects.

Bo leaned down and spoke into Holly's ear, stirring the curls she'd pinned away from her face.

"Ready for some shopping?" he asked.

She nodded, smiling up at him. He'd been hoping that they might snag some press attention today, on this little field trip to the baby shop. Kill two birds with one stone, right? Patronize a small business in town that needed attention and show off his family-man side at the same time.

The shopkeeper seemed thrilled to have Thunder Canyon's newest and most visible couple in her store, and she showed them everything from cradles to hand-sewn receiving blankets.

Holly was on cloud nine, picturing Hopper wearing a cute yellow sleeper with pandas sewn all over it.

Without even looking at the price tag, Bo said, "We'll take it. And how about this, too?" he asked Holly, pointing to a rainbow of other displayed sleepers.

He must've seen the adoring sheen in her gaze, because before she could tell him not to spend too much, he asked the owner for those, as well. Plus the rose-festooned white wicker cradle Holly had run her hand over on the way into the store. Plus everything else her baby would need that was within sight.

As the owner rang everything up and arranged a special delivery to Bo's ranch, Holly pulled him aside. She kept a smile on her face because she was fully aware that the reporter was still outside the store window, along with a few other citizens who'd gathered.

"Bo," she began.

"Before you say anything, the baby deserves every bit of it. So do you."

Then he kissed her on the forehead again, but this time, his lips stayed against her skin for a moment longer than any business arrangement would require.

Holly's body flared with yearning as his breath warmed her skin. An old-fashioned sign of affection.

And the more Bo acted like a gallant, the more she wanted him.

By the time they left the store, a small crowd was waiting outside.

A college-age girl said, "Go, Bo!"

The rest clapped while the reporter took another picture. As Bo protectively put his arm around Holly's shoulders and led her away, toward their parked vehicles, the flash seemed to haunt them.

"Let's get you back for some rest," he said.

Holly had driven her pickup to town, separate from Bo since they were both on different timetables, and as they climbed into their own vehicles, she said, "I'm not tired."

"You should be, after such an expedition."

He smiled, closed his door while making sure she started her pickup and drove off ahead of him before he, too, headed for his ranch.

It was only after they entered his house that the façade of Public Bo wore off. In fact, as he tossed his coat and hat on the entry rack, he was relatively distant, just as he'd been yesterday while she'd moved in. But Holly had chalked that up to them doing their own tasks—him bringing in her boxes, her arranging her room and then lying down when her back had started aching a tad.

He was already walking toward his study in the back of the house when she stopped him.

"Bo?"

She wasn't sure why she didn't want him to leave in such a hurry.

He paused in the foyer. "Can I get you something? What do you need?"

What did she *need?*

She refrained. It was hard, but she kept her most private thoughts to herself and said, "You don't have to get me anything. You got me enough at that shop, and thank you—thank you so much—but..."

"I already said that you and Hopper deserve that and more."

He began to leave again, as if he was in some kind of

hurry to get away from her, just as he'd been ever since their wedding night.

"I went to my practitioner's appointment today," she said, wanting to say *something* to him, even if it wasn't what her heart wanted her to be speaking.

Her doctor's comment really halted him, but he didn't turn to her, so she couldn't see the expression on his face.

"Nothing's wrong with me or the baby," she quickly added. "The doctor just told me that she wants me to gain some weight. She's always on me about that. I…just thought you'd want to know I was there, in case anyone mentions it to you."

"Why didn't you remind me you were going?" he asked in a voice so soft that she didn't know what to make of it.

"About the appointment?" Should she have? "I knew you'd be busy. And I've been seeing the doctor on my own for a while."

He stayed turned away from her for a few more seconds. Holly could hear her heartbeat in her ears.

Finally, he faced her, his features relaxed and casual. Typical Bo.

Had she expected anything else?

"If it's okay with you," he said. "I'd like to go with you next time."

"Of course. I should've thought about it. My husband would be interested in my sonograms and health, and you'd be free to go to the appointments now that we've come clean about our relationship to the public."

Something—betrayal?—flashed over his gaze, but it was there and gone, so she didn't know if it'd only been a trick of her mind.

But why would her words affect him in such a way? Bo wasn't really the proud father-to-be that the public knew.

And his next comment proved it.

"It would look good if I was involved with the day-to-day stuff with you and Hopper," he said.

Even though his gaze stayed on her belly—just like the time they'd been in the bridal shop and he'd stopped himself from touching her belly—he turned around, going for the hallway.

Taking a little part of her with him, too, even though she hadn't wanted to give it over.

Chapter Eight

Another interview down, many more to go, Bo thought when he returned to his house that night, closing the door behind him so that the gurgle from the creek and the cold air stayed outside. The sun had pretty much disappeared since this afternoon, leaving the slight threat of rain behind, so there was also a trace of sulfur and restlessness in the atmosphere that didn't belong in a house.

Without meaning to, he listened, hoping to hear Holly somewhere. But everything was quiet, only the ticking of a clock from the living room chopping the atmosphere into bits.

"Holly?" he asked.

No answer.

Was she already in bed?

He could just about see her: blond curls spread over

her pillow, an arm thrown over her head, her lips open while she breathed in and out, the clouded moon coming in from a window to paint her skin smooth and pale.

Bo's heart rate got a little tangled up at thinking about how he would love to brush any stray hairs back from her face, then lean down, his mouth against her cheek, then against her lips…

He tugged off his coat and hat, but when he tossed them and missed the rack by the door altogether, he didn't bother to pick either of them up.

Later. He would do it later.

Right now, he just wanted to walk by Holly's room, to see if she was in there. To reassure himself that he hadn't chased her off after how he'd acted earlier.

When he came to her closed door, he paused, his fingertips against the wood. Inside, he heard the low murmur of the TV.

So she had stayed around, even after he'd acted so brusque about her going to the doctor alone. He'd seen the bewilderment written all over her face after he'd shown her too much of what he'd been hiding in himself, thoughts that didn't even have any business being there.

Hell, why *had* he been disappointed that she'd gone to a prenatal appointment by herself? Because it might make people wonder why a husband wouldn't be there, looking at those pictures they took of a baby inside a woman's belly?

A sonogram. That's what they were called. And damn him if he felt a little stung because Holly hadn't *wanted* him there to see the baby.

Now that he knew she was home, he stepped away from her room, intending to go to his own. But he didn't even make it that far, because the door to his second guestroom had been left open, and he could see the packages from their baby boutique shopping trip piled inside.

From a cradle to a bunch of little itty bitty baby clothing, he'd bought just about everything in that store because he thought it would make Holly smile. He thought her child might be happier, too, if Mommy felt that way.

Scanning the walls, Bo wondered what the baby might like, as far as decorations went. Pandas, like he'd seen on that one sleeper outfit? Teddy bears?

That might be fun. Old-fashioned bear pictures. And would the baby like pastel colors—blue or pink?—over his or her walls? Bo could get right to painting them, after the election stopped demanding all of his time.

Then again, he and Holly hadn't talked about any of this. There just hadn't been a spare moment, with the wedding, his campaign...

The urge to go to her, whether she was sleeping or not, pulled at him. And it wasn't just because they needed more talk.

No. He just...

Wanted to see her again before he called it a night.

Resisting, Bo left the nursery and went straight to his room, not even daring to look back toward Holly's. This was a fine position to be in—wanting his "wife." His body needed to wise up, to know the difference between duty and lust.

And it was his duty to keep Holly safe now, especially from him. Damn it, he'd taken advantage of her situation. She really *was* young, and he just hoped this pseudo-marriage didn't mess up the rest of her life… or the baby's.

But when he came to his door, he saw something taped to it. A picture.

A sonogram photo of a tiny being all curled up, his or her fists bunched.

Hopper?

Bo took down the picture, smiling, but then he realized what he was doing.

He was acting like a proud dad when that wasn't the case.

As he tucked the picture into his nightstand, he took one last glance at it. He'd have to detach himself from his not-really family now, because somehow, Holly and the baby had become sewn into the fabric of his days, even though she wasn't his wife.

And the baby wasn't his child.

Bo shut the drawer, but he still heard the hum of Holly's TV down the hall, and he tried his best to unstitch himself from his houseguest.

Trouble was, with every thread, he wondered if he was going to become a little more undone himself.

After Rose Friedel had gotten wind of Bo's baby boutique spree, she'd hit upon an idea for another rally over a week later, with the election only about two weeks away.

Hence, here they all were, Holly thought, bundled in her coat, scarf and gloves as the dusk-hushed air nipped at her cheeks.

She and Bo were standing in the flatbed of a truck in front of Cora's Baby Haven, the shop where she and her husband had held that now infamous spree. It'd become a symbol of sorts for his campaign—a struggling small business that had the potential to be raised from the ashes of Thunder Canyon's economy. The reporter from the lifestyles magazine had already featured her pictures on her publication's blog, and the mention of the shop had increased business.

Then again, the reporter had also posted that photo of Bo and Holly, just after Holly had almost slipped on the walkway. "A Prince to the Rescue," it had said underneath.

Holly had looked at it, remembering how the reporter had mentioned Charles and Di, and she'd felt the lie growing that much more.

Every day the lies escalated, just like the chants from the crowd right now.

"Bo! Bo!"

Holly's heart copied every pump of their fists.

Bo!

Bo!

Too bad these slams of desire were getting stronger every single night, too, after Holly and Bo retired for the evening, going to their separate rooms. She would stare at the ceiling, holding her breath, wishing she could hear him outside her door, just as she'd heard him that night over a week ago.

Her TV had been playing an old movie on low volume, but his whispered voice had come to her loud and clear, anyway.

"Holly?" he'd asked.

She had wanted to answer, but her tongue had been too tied. If she opened her mouth, it would be to invite him in.

Then what?

Even now, as her body responded to every "Bo!", Holly knew. She wouldn't have been able to stop what would have surely happened that night.

As she watched him waiting for the crowd to wear itself out, one thumb hitched into the belt loop of his jeans, his stance so achingly masculine and laconic, that same desire traveled over Holly's skin.

And under it.

He glanced back at her, just like a politician husband sharing a grand moment with his wife. And, for a flicker of time, a snap of connected understanding, it was real.

She was proud of Bo. So proud that her chest constricted at the sight of his success and the good future he was going to bring this town.

Absently, she rested her hand on her sweater-covered tummy, where the baby had really started to show by now. All Holly's curves were beginning to pop, mostly because Bo had started to become vigilant about keeping her well fed.

"Doctor's orders," he always said just before getting that tender look that seemed to disappear before it lasted too long.

His gaze softened now, too, as he glanced at her belly. Holly wished he could see that it was okay to touch her.

Wasn't it okay?

Couldn't it be?

When the crowd settled down, Bo wrapped up tonight's speech, flashes from cameras lighting him like more pulses that echoed in Holly.

"The time is coming," he said, his voice quieter than usual. "We've done our best in these endeavors so far.

But I'm going to ask you for one more thing, folks. I need that extra push only you can give to me. Just one more heave-ho behind our campaign wagon. One more huge effort down this last mile—"

A male voice emerged from the group. "One more trick to get him across the finish line!"

Everyone froze, including Holly and Bo. A bad vibe skittered up Holly's spine.

The speaker didn't sound like a supporter.

Rose Friedel even sidled up to Holly, taking up her side, as if sensing the same.

But Bo didn't lose his cool. He merely smiled at the rest of his supporters and shrugged modestly, as if communicating that there was one in every crowd.

The speaker continued before Bo could talk again.

"Tell us—how far would you go to be mayor? Would you even stage a fake marriage so that—"

The crowd's voices drowned out the heckler.

Rose held Holly's hand, but Bo was already talking into the microphone, his voice graveled with that same grit Holly had only heard during his most emotional moments.

"Don't speak against my wife and child."

He had his finger raised, and it seemed as if he was ready to bolt into the audience, taking this up face-to-face with the so-far anonymous heckler.

But he was acting, Holly told herself. He was only acting like this was an affront. Like he...cared.

Still, it seemed as if he truly was angry as his skin turned ruddy, his jaw tight.

His voice even rougher.

"I don't mind your coming here to give me a little run for my money," he said to the faceless aggressor.

"But when it comes to my family, back off, understand? Holly is…"

He cut himself off, staring at the ground, as if gathering himself. Rose put her arm around Holly, whose heart was beating its way up her throat.

"My wife is more than a man like me could've ever hoped for," Bo finally said. "She puts others far above herself. She's kind and optimistic and so beautiful inside and out that I thank my lucky stars every single night that she decided to even give me the time of day."

She wished he meant it. God, she wished it so badly, and she had no idea how that had happened. How she'd let it.

"So, sir," Bo continued, getting control of his tone, pushing his cowboy hat back a little on his head. "I'm partial to giving second chances, especially since I truly believe that you spoke in error. But know this."

He lowered his voice to a pitch Holly had never heard before and hoped she would never hear again.

"I won't tolerate another ugly word about the people I hold dear. Not a word. Understand?"

His supporters exploded into cheers, which quickly transformed to more fervent chants of "Bo! Bo!" than ever before.

He stared down the heckler, who'd been isolated by a group of supporters as the guy, who wore a straw hat, parted the crowd on his way out of the rally. Then Bo turned, making eye contact with Rose, who guided Holly to a mini set of stairs that led off of the truck and toward Bo's waiting black SUV that would take them to campaign headquarters.

Bo hadn't looked at Holly though. Not even close.

And she was glad for that, because she hadn't wanted him to see how shaken she was. How…

She didn't know. Didn't know anything anymore.

After Bo sat in the backseat with Holly, shutting the door with a bang, Rose drove them away. He still didn't look at Holly, even as she finally summoned the strength to want him to.

What had this all meant?

And why had it sounded as if…

Stop it, she told herself, holding her stomach, just like she could shield the baby from her thoughts. *Don't talk yourself into thinking that Bo was doing anything more than campaigning.*

If she started to believe that he cared, she would only get stomped on again when she'd barely even repaired herself from Alan's betrayal.

And she feared it would hurt much worse this time, because Alan wasn't Bo.

As they drove, no one—not Bo, Holly nor Rose—had anything to say until they arrived at headquarters, where they ensconced themselves in the back office with the door closed.

The lighthearted Bo was all gone, leaving a pacing, barely contained man in his place.

"That was Arthur Swinton's work," he said.

Holly sat in the chair in front of his desk, her limbs weak. It was as if she was watching everything from a near distance, and if she hadn't known what was going on, she would've said that Bo genuinely was furious.

Rose sure treated him as if he needed some assuaging. She had the tone of a lion tamer.

"It's over, Bo, and you handled the situation like a pro."

"A pro?"

He halted. Then it happened.

He looked at Holly.

Her stomach flipped when she saw something similar there to what she'd witnessed the night she'd gone to the doctor without telling him.

Something heartfelt and profound.

Something…

Holly felt Rose focus on her now, too, and when she glanced at the older woman, she read her expression quite clearly.

Astonishment.

Don't dare *think it. Don't start believing that Rose believes there's more to this marriage than fakery.*

Bo spoke. "I'm not only going to wring Swinton's neck for planting that howler, but for having that fool cast any dirt whatsoever on Holly and the baby. My family's off-limits."

"Bo, calm down," Rose said. "You—"

"Enough." Bo raised his hands. "Matters have gone too far. I shouldn't have ever brought Holly and the baby into this, and maybe now's the time to call off this entire charade. I won't see them dragged through any more mud."

"And lose the election?" Rose asked. "Because that's what would happen."

An expression of such loss crossed Bo's face that Holly flashed to the night when he had talked about his uncle's and Andre Julen's murders—his passion for what was right. His agonizing determination to make sure nothing unjust ever happened again in Thunder Canyon. His plans to make everything better.

"Don't you call anything off," Holly said. "Don't you quit on me."

He lowered his hands, as if hardly believing what he was hearing.

God, had she really said that?

"Quit on…you?" he asked.

Exposed—completely, utterly revealed for what she had come to feel for this man.

That flush attacked her again. "Quit on *any* of us."

The lie didn't sit well, but this wasn't the time to complicate the situation. She wouldn't let him hear what was in her heart…not all of it. But she couldn't let him sabotage his campaign because of one setback.

Holly scooted forward in her seat. "When you first came to me with this proposal, I thought you were full of it. Then…"

"Then…?" It was a rough whisper.

Holly swallowed, feeling as if she was getting in further by the moment.

"Then," she said, "I started to believe in what you stood for. I saw that you might be a lot of smooth talk on the outside, but inside?" She touched her heart. "Here? You had everything that counts. Everything we need here in Thunder Canyon."

He looked at her, into her, as if he was asking, "Everything *we* need? Or everything *you* need?"

A slow melt made Holly liquid, made her all his.

She couldn't deny it any more—not only did she believe in Bo, she'd fallen for him. Hard. Fast.

Undoubtedly.

Inside her belly, the baby jostled around, as if he or she was snuggling up to her realizations. Heat pricked her eyes as she glanced away from Bo.

Love. She'd fallen in love with her husband of convenience just when it was the *least* convenient.

She heard Bo moving around, going to the office door, opening it, but she didn't look up. Not even when Rose rested a comforting hand on her shoulder, as if she'd recognized Holly's pain.

As if she was sorry it had happened, too.

As Bo drove home, Holly remained quiet in the passenger seat, staring out the window at the moonlit grasses, the passing fences.

The silence was killing him, especially after tonight, when there was so much that should be said. So much that couldn't be voiced because it would change everything.

And change wasn't what *they* needed. Not the two of them.

"I was thinking of painting the baby's room the day after the election," he said, hoping to ease the tension with business. Plans upon plans. "We can use that duckling yellow color you saw in the catalog."

About a week ago, he'd approached her about the décor, and she'd also loved the old-fashioned bear idea, although he got the feeling that she was just being adaptable, seeing as the baby wouldn't live in the nursery for too long.

A pang hit him, but it made no sense when, all this time, he'd known they would go.

He injected some levity into his tone. "Painting might console me if I lose."

More silence, and it gave him enough time to realize that he'd meant losing the election. But now, loss had another meaning for him.

Holly. Hopper.

So what if he kept thinking he saw glimmers of affection in Holly every time he glanced at her? Or if she'd seemed to reveal so much more tonight when she'd talked about believing in him…

He didn't say anything more, because he had been the one who'd said too damned much earlier, ripping himself open and defending Holly to that heckler who'd crashed the rally.

Bo gripped the steering wheel. He'd sure sounded like a man in love with Holly. But even worse, her faith in him touched him where no one had ever gone before.

Over the line, he thought. He'd definitely crossed a boundary tonight, and it had to stop here, while he still had a chance of scrambling back over to sane territory.

Holly finally responded to his nursery comments, although she was still facing the window, not him.

"I'm on board with whatever colors you like."

Helpless as to what to do, Bo kept driving. And when they finally, thankfully entered the house, Holly didn't even take off her coat. She went straight for the wraparound porch, and Bo took this as a hint that she wanted to be alone.

Had everything become too much for her?

Great—here, he'd told her that marrying him would alleviate her stress, not multiply it.

He went to the kitchen, but it wasn't because he was hungry. He'd noticed that Holly hadn't eaten since lunch, so he put together a turkey sandwich on wheat bread with all the trimmings and took the tin plate plus a glass of orange juice to the porch. After he delivered it, he would scoot, giving them both the privacy and recovery they sorely needed.

He found her sitting in a cedar chair, her coat bundled around her, the moon shining down on her blond curls and twisting his heart into swerves he'd never be able to negotiate, even if he tried.

"Here you go," he said, sliding the plate onto her lap and waiting for her to grab it before he let go. He set the juice on the wide armrest next to her.

"I'm not very hungry."

"Your doctor would disagree."

The creek burbled by, providing all the chatter that they couldn't seem to conjure up until Holly thanked him, as if seeking the easiest way out of this and hoping he would leave without more fuss.

But she didn't touch her food. Was she expecting him to go first?

Well, he would oblige her, just as soon as he was assured that she was comfortable.

"It's cold out here," he said. "I can get you a blanket. Or maybe you should just—"

"You and your manners."

He tucked his hands below his armpits under his coat, barring himself until he realized what he was doing and loosened up.

"What's wrong with being a gentleman?" he asked.

"It's just that a polite gentleman is all you are when we get out of the public's gaze. When we're out there—" she motioned toward the world "—you're more of an actual family man, closer and more affectionate, than you are here."

What?

She sighed. "I'm sorry. I knew what I was signing

up for. It's just that..." She leaned back her head and rested it against the chair, so weary that it stung him. "I'm tired of the playacting, Bo."

He tried not to fall into the hole in the ground that had suddenly opened beneath his boots.

Tired...? Playacting...?

This wasn't good, having her say these things. Wasn't good at all.

"Then I was right," he said. "When I told you that I should call things off before they go too far, I was right."

She stood, the plate and sandwich falling to the deck with a clang, and Bo dropped his hands down to his sides when he saw the look on her face.

Fiery.

He realized that she wasn't just angry at him—this was a woman who knew what she wanted, and though he'd seen flashes before of what that might be, he still couldn't believe it.

Him? She wanted her not-really husband?

His common sense told him to walk away. To run. But he stayed rooted, each second like a ball bouncing down a stairway, faster, heavier, coming to some kind of end.

"Bo," she said, "I don't think you understand what I'm telling you."

"Holly..."

"I said I'm tired of playacting, but I'm not talking about the charade." She took a big breath, then blew it out. "I've had it with trying to hide what's really going on in me...what I'm feeling."

"Let's just go inside." Maybe she would rethink what she was saying if he could stall long enough...

"Would you just listen? I saw something in your defense of me this evening, at the rally. What you said… What you told that guy…" She straightened her spine. "There's more to this marriage than a sham, and we both know it."

Oh, damn—there it was.

Adrenaline infused him, making his heartbeat feel like an electric saw, spinning until it was nothing but a dangerous, cutting buzz that split him down the middle.

Half of him wanted to take her into his arms and never let go, kissing her until she had to gasp for breath, feeling her in places that he'd made himself forget during the stillness of each night, when he dreamed about her.

But the other half…

It was this part that made him walk away, following the urgent demands of his survival instincts—the common sense that had kept him a bachelor for so long, a man whose heart was still intact.

She followed him into the house, slamming the porch door behind her until the glass rattled.

"You get back here, Bo."

"You'll come to your right mind in the morning, after we slumber this off."

"Just like every night, right? Don't you tell me that you're not thinking about me while you try to sleep down the hallway."

He was in that hallway now, but he could hear her on his tail.

Damn it.

As he passed her room, he could smell her: the honeyed scent that had consumed him every day since she'd come back to Thunder Canyon.

Dizzy with it, he slowed, just as if the heaviness of her scent dragged him down.

Lifted him up.

She caught him, grabbing him by the coat and pulling him back.

"We're getting this out in the open and we're doing it now," Holly said. "Because we're not putting a premature end to this marriage, this 'charade' or whatever you want to call it."

He was almost to his room…

But Holly was a willful one, and she tugged him so hard that he spun around.

And before he knew it, she was kissing him.

At the end of his rope, Bo couldn't do anything but bury his fingers into her curls, feeling the silk of them. The heaven of them.

And he kissed his wife right back, every blazing cell of his body hers.

Chapter Nine

As Holly sank against Bo, she told herself that she had only chased him down because of those damned pregnancy hormones—and because of being with him 24/7, night in and night out.

Both had driven her to the edge—to rash action and fevered need. *They* were the reasons that every inch of her body was churning, flipping, rearranging in such a rush and burn that she could barely move as Bo's lips sipped at hers, a combination of gentleness and insistence.

Of worship and heat.

He kissed her as if it was the first and last time he'd ever kissed anyone—as if he needed to handle her like a breakable creature while he held himself back, refusing to harm her.

But she was already breaking as he kissed her, his

fingers caught in her hair, his breathing ragged as he ran his mouth over hers.

Then he pulled back from her, recovering from the desperation of their kiss.

"Don't stop," she said, not realizing that she'd voiced it until it echoed off the walls.

And she was glad she'd told him. Glad this was finally happening.

"We *need* to stop right now," he whispered. "Or else I won't be able to. I don't know if we should even be doing th—"

She gripped the lapels of his coat. She knew what she needed.

Knew what he did, too, no matter what her common sense was telling her.

"No stopping." The scent of him made her reel: the suede of his coat, the musk of his skin.

There would be consequences for this, but Holly didn't care what they were. For a woman who'd based her life on plans and expectations, there was freedom in letting go and knowing that she could take whatever life tossed her way, in living this moment with him. In wrapping her arms around Bo's neck and pulling him back down to her for another kiss.

He groaned, and she felt it rumble through her, too, as she opened up to him.

Their kiss deepened, his tongue stroking hers, slow, languorous. The sensual rhythm built in her, tug by wicked tug. It expanded inside her, a throb that pulsed upward, down, making her swell and ache.

She slid one of her hands under his coat, gliding her palm up his muscled chest, where she lingered over every contour.

Hot skin over firm muscle. The shape of a man.

A man she wanted more than any other.

Bewilderment tried to jam its way into her. Hadn't Alan been the love of her life?

Or was she meant to be with Bo, her convenient husband, instead?

None of this had been planned, and it was exciting, stimulating her like a cool breeze over skin that had turned to flames of need, prickles of desire.

As she ran her hand down, over his ribs, Bo sucked in a sharp breath. The sound sparked even more passion in Holly, and she pushed at his coat, working it off of him in a near frenzy.

"Last chance," he murmured against her.

"I'll take it."

She tossed his coat to the ground, then started on the snaps of his shirt, yanking it off of him until she got to bare flesh.

With his shirt tangled over her arm, she pulled back from him, just to see.

Just to enjoy all the more.

He was beautiful in the angle of light that seeped into the hallway from the living room. As golden as nostalgic days bathed in perfect memory—days Bo wanted to bring back to all of them.

Muscles, cut and smooth. Broad shoulders, toned arms and chest.

Holly reached out to touch his waist, the hard line of it leading to the ridges of his abs. Then she pulled her hand back, shyness overcoming her, even after all her bravado.

He lifted his hand, coasting his knuckles over her

cheekbone, as if assuaging her, caring for her feelings even now.

Affection flooded her, and she shucked off her coat. It thudded to the floor as she went for her sweater, pulling it over her head, static snapping at her, crackling in the air along with the tension between them just before she discarded that piece of clothing, too.

A few hairs whisked against her face, floating, and Bo smiled, his hand going to her head to smooth down the rebellious strands.

But there was no taming the rebel in *her,* and she turned her head to kiss the inside of his wrist, grabbing his arm with both hands. She slid one of them upward, over the mound of his biceps while she nuzzled his palm.

His chest rose and fell, and she knew it was because he was trying to keep himself under control, letting her take the lead, still reluctant to do more with her.

She would change that. Bo felt something for her, whether or not he would admit it. Whether or not he was willing to risk the same chances she was all too revved up to take.

She roamed her hand down his chest, toward his belt buckle. His belly muscles jerked.

"Holly—"

"I want this."

"And what about…"

He gestured toward her tummy.

Warmth—not the sexual heat that had been coursing through her, but tender, sighing *warmth*—surrounded her heart.

Even now, he was thinking about her baby. Thinking about her, beyond just being a short-time stand. A woman to take to bed.

"The doctor knew I'd be on my honeymoon," she said, breathy. "So she told me it'd be fine. Just…gentle, okay? Slow. Easy."

When she tugged at his belt, he exhaled, his breath shakier than she could've ever predicted. She undid his buckle, then the top button of his fly. He was already hard—she could feel that as her knuckles brushed against him.

Bo stifled a grunt, and she reached up to undo her bra. With the garment off, her breasts felt full, sensitive, and when Holly took Bo's hands in hers and brought them up to her chest, the mere touch made her gasp.

He started to take his hands away, but she kept them against her, cupping her. She bit her lip, increasing the pressure, urging him to rest his thumbs over her nipples, moaning as he gently circled there.

A stiffness emerged between her legs, moistness. Readiness.

She brought a hand to the back of his head, and he understood, bending to her, his palms sliding to her back as he rubbed his lips against a nipple.

A craving for him almost decimated Holly, especially when he licked at her, getting her even more stimulated.

He kept gently exploring her breasts with his mouth, his fingers. Meanwhile, Holly pushed down her skirt, stepped out of it and then her panties.

Running his lips down her body, he came to her belly. Slowly, he got to his knees, fitting his hands to her roundness.

"You're everything I could ever imagine," he said.

He was saying this to *her,* the woman who'd been left behind by another. To the baby.

To the family they'd become.

Overwhelmed, she led him to her room, where the bed waited, white and wide under the moonlight coming in through the window.

After taking off his boots, he laid her on the mattress, staring down at her with so much adoration on his face that tears came to her eyes.

She raised herself up, pulling him down and guiding him to his back. She would be careful, so careful.

They faced each other, lying on their sides, and she skimmed the bulge in his jeans. She could feel the tip of him through the denim.

He cursed under his breath and, panting, Holly unbuttoned the rest of his fly and brought him all the way out. The breath left her as she held him in her palm, his entire, stiff length.

When she stroked him, bringing him to an arching, groaning point of no return, she watched his face—the play of emotion, the pained bliss of escalation.

Happy. She was making him happy, and she could do the same thing night after night like no other woman could, because she couldn't imagine him in more ecstasy than this.

She loved him with her hands, explored him, made him all hers until he clasped the back of her hip.

"Yes," she said, raising her leg slightly so that she parted for him, then positioning herself so that her tummy wasn't between them.

He slid his tip against her most intimate part, teasing her, pressing against the center of her until the pressure drove her wild.

She felt like she was spring-loaded, ready to fly open with just one more nudge of his erection against her, one more…

With a burst, she expanded, cried out, all of her scattered to the winds that seemed to whip through her. High, low, she was everywhere as Bo slipped himself into her.

Velvet, slick, she gasped as her orgasm made her clench around him.

They moved in leisurely rhythm, a long cadence that flowed like a sinuous river, running, then after a while, picking up speed bit by bit until Holly felt as if her cells were tumbling over each other, roaring, pushing—

As he stiffened, finding release, she dug her fingers into him, watching his face, loving how she made him feel just as much as she…

Loved him.

Their breath evened out, unmatched now, and she waited, listening to him, wondering what he would say.

Then he pulled her closer, his chest against hers, making words unnecessary.

While she fell asleep against him, giddier than she'd ever been in her life, she dreamed of ice cream trucks, a green yard where the musical songs floated over a sunset breeze.

Yet, this time in the fantasy, Bo was there, too, right by her side, the man she'd been meant to find.

After putting himself in order, Bo came back to bed, where he held Holly again. He even took the covers and wrapped them around them, just like a cocoon.

But weren't cocoons meant to be broken? Didn't other things emerge?

More beautiful things, he thought, though with every beat of his heart, he wondered what could come of this.

What they'd done.

He looked down at her, lying so sweetly in the crook of his arm, her lashes fanned over her cheeks, her lips so soft that he wanted to kiss them again.

And again.

The only matter stopping him was the guilt.

Who would've guessed it? This experience had shaken him more completely than any other time. It had ripped him to shreds, making the scraps of him free fall to the ground, where the thrusts of his emotions destroyed him so thoroughly that he wasn't sure he could ever find himself again.

Not after her.

Holly sighed in her sleep, snuggling against him, a smile taking over her mouth as she nestled her hand just beneath his ear. Even a simple touch like that had the power to get him going again, his belly clenching, heat rushing to his groin.

But there was also something rushing to his heart, and every instinct that had kept him intact told him to flush it out.

He couldn't fall in love with her. That hadn't been part of their deal. Sure, he could keep all the other components of his bargain with Holly, but this...?

This, he hadn't expected.

This, he hadn't been able to resist when Holly had made it so clear that she wanted to include the marriage bed in their bargain, and he hadn't been able to stop himself from giving in and putting a smile on her face that she was even wearing during sleep.

She'd found happiness in making *him* happy…

As she stirred against him again, he automatically took her in his arms. An impulse. A necessity.

His downfall.

He began to ease away from her, just so he could leave, get her out of his system, think a little.

Think.

But then she opened her eyes and he was just as lost as he'd been that first time, when he'd turned around like a fool and kissed her, the beginning of this end.

While she flashed those big blues at him, Bo turned to jelly.

"Hello," she said, her voice raspy.

"Holly…"

He couldn't finish when she wiggled closer to him, the baby bump curving against his stomach. Absently, he rested his fingertips against the baby's curve.

When he felt a kick, he was a total goner.

Holly quietly laughed. "Hopper's at it. I read that after sex, a baby can get more lively."

Sex. It didn't seem to describe what had gone on here, although it was the best he'd ever had, no matter how you put it. It'd mingled the explosions of his body with something more—a rising sensation that went beyond any climax. A closeness, a moment when he'd taken her all the way into him and felt that, for the first time in his life, he'd found a completion above anything else.

Intimacy.

Even the word scared the tar out of him, and his pulse shuddered. Fight or flight.

Survival.

But there he was, keeping his hand against her belly, hoping to feel another kick, another sign of the life that was soon to join them.

And what kind of life would it be, after their deal was up? Would the child despise Bo for leaving them, after he or she was old enough to know the meaning of desertion?

Or…

Good God—would Holly think that tonight meant that there'd be no annulment?

Damn, he wished his brain had possessed the power to trump his body tonight. When he'd proposed to her, he'd only been thinking about the campaign, the good of the many versus the good of the few.

But, for some reason, Holly and her baby seemed far more important than any big crusade now, and that wasn't what he'd proposed when he'd offered up this marriage to her.

Think man, think.

Bo rested his cheek against her head. He hated himself for losing his mind when she'd pulled him in for a kiss, but he *would* live up to his end of the deal, show her that he would always be there. There had to be a way to do that while not hurting her.

"You need sleep," he said, getting to his elbow. But as he did, it gave him a better view of her, with those tossed curls and the lazy posture of a woman who liked to snuggle.

At his distance, a look of confusion covered her expression, and it was beyond Bo not to appease her.

He adjusted their positions so that he was sitting and holding her feet in his hands. During a few idle moments in the office, he'd done a search on pregnancy, and he'd read that foot massages were a pretty popular thing for an expectant mother.

After combing his thumbs down her insteps, he was proven correct when Holly sighed, curving her arms over her head.

Unfortunately, that highlighted her breasts, showing off how full they were, even if they'd probably been smallish before, with Holly's slender figure. It showed off the dark pink of her nipples, which looked like cherries.

He remembered how they'd felt in his mouth—smooth, the nubs of them like little stems for his tongue to play with.

She yawned, even as she said, "I'm not sleepy."

When he concentrated on one foot, applying pressure with both thumbs now, she wiggled her hips.

Careful, he thought, and it wasn't just because it was best not to work her up again. It was because *he* needed the warning, too.

But as Holly closed her eyes, her breath becoming shallow, Bo's chest warmed. He lavished a look on her—one that he felt free to give, now that she couldn't see it—and thought about what it might be like if he were a different man.

And if he could change and become that man for anyone, it would be Holly. It would be for the baby.

But he wouldn't change, not for a marriage that would no doubt turn sour one day, just as he'd seen his parents' do.

As Holly drifted off, Bo tucked her in, staying by her side and watching her for far too long before he left the room, shutting the door softly, but firmly, behind him.

* * *

Morning came through Holly's window with the song of a bird, a bright stream of sunshine and the warm breath of the central heat coming through her bedroom vent.

She stretched, her skin feeling…different.

Awake. Slightly sore, as if…

Bo.

Reaching out next to her, she grasped air, then turned on her side to discover the reason.

No Bo.

She sat up, and as the air hit her skin, she pulled up the sheets, covering her bare chest. Her breasts were sensitive, too, but in a good way, and she remembered Bo's mouth on her, sucking, bringing her to places she'd forgotten existed.

Where was he?

As she started to get out of bed, she saw a piece of paper on the pillow. A note.

Gone to the office already. Didn't want to wake you. See you for dinner?

No signature, no xxx's or ooo's… No sense of what had gone on between them last night.

Then again, Bo was a man, and how many guys did she know who left xxx's and ooo's?

Even so, hadn't he kissed her with all the desire that she'd felt, too? Hadn't they…

Holly wiped a hand over her face, thinking for a second that maybe she'd imagined it. But he'd been in her room. The note had proven it.

Heavy with doubt, she got out of the bed and pulled on a thick terrycloth robe.

Had Bo just left a note because he wanted to flee from her room?

Did he regret being with her?

When she opened her door, the aroma of coffee and breakfast hung in the air. She looked down at the floor, where there was another piece of paper.

An arrow.

She cupped her hand over her belly, following the arrow to another one, then another, until she got to the kitchen and the refrigerator.

Inside, she discovered breakfast laid out on a tray: a glass of orange juice that had been protected by a baggie. A plastic-covered plate featuring a big omelet smothered in grated, unmelted cheese.

There was a note here, as well.

Warm in the microwave—doc's orders.

This time there was a smiley face at the bottom, next to a scribbled "Bo."

"Not exactly xxx's and ooo's," Holly said out loud to her unborn child, "but it's an improvement."

She took out the tray, thinking that she could joke with Hopper, but did her baby sense that she was unsettled by Bo's notes? That she was disappointed that he hadn't woken her up with a kiss?

That heaviness pushed down on her as she warmed up her breakfast. But then she started to wonder if some men, especially commitment-shy ones like Bo, were better with gestures, like making her breakfast and taking care of her in that way, rather than with endearments and good-morning kisses.

She tried not to think about how this caretaking still smacked of the playacting husband. Tried not to wonder if Bo had backed off because…

Oh, God, had she been terrible in bed?

Had she let him down?

After all, Bo was older, more experienced. There was also the chance that he might've just taken pity on her since she'd come on to him like a cat in heat.

Did he regret their whole marriage?

As her paranoia snowballed, she walked toward the bathroom to get ready for a day of light work—she was supposed to make some arrangements for a Halloween fundraiser at the resort.

But the questions kept at her.

Alan had left her because she'd done something wrong with him. Could it be that she was a walking case of failure? Even after she'd spent so much of her life trying to avoid screwing up, here she was, a two-time loser…

Maybe she should call Erika, but as soon as Holly thought it, she quashed the idea. Her friend had been afraid this would happen. Plus, she was knee deep in her wedding arrangements. No way would Holly lay this on her.

But just she was gargling with mouthwash after brushing her teeth, she heard her phone ring, and she rushed to her room, riffling through her coat, which Bo must've put in here after they'd stripped in the hallway last night.

When she found the phone, she answered. "Hello?"

"Holly?"

It wasn't Erika, as she'd hoped.

"This is Rose."

A bolt of fear hit Holly. Why would Rose be calling?

"Is Bo...?" she asked.

His manager must've heard the worry in Holly's tone, because she quickly said, "Nothing's wrong. I only thought I'd call to check up on you after...that rally."

It took Holly a second to calm her pulse, to remember that there'd been things that had occurred last night besides her and Bo getting cozy.

Things like the heckler and the moment in the campaign office when Rose had placed her hand on Holly's shoulder, as if telling her that she knew everything that was going on between the fake couple.

"I'm doing fine," Holly said, putting that sunshine brightness into her voice. The sparkly tone that had carried her through so many years of attempting to please everyone, first and foremost among them herself.

"Good." Rose hesitated.

Weird, because Holly didn't think a woman like Rose Friedel paused in much of anything.

Then the woman continued. "I'm concerned, Holly. And I thought you might need an ear to hear you out."

No use lying to the woman. She was as sharp as a tack.

"Bo and I are working through things," she said carefully. "There have been some...curveballs in our deal."

"I thought so. I know what you said last night, about him staying the course. But I wondered if you really meant it—that he shouldn't dissolve this marriage. Because matters are going to only build during the next couple of weeks, Holly. Are you ready for that?"

Build in what way? Holly wanted to ask. With the politics?

Or with her and Bo?

She wanted to tell Rose about how he'd looked at her in the moonlight, how she would bet her life on the fact that there'd been something to his gaze, his touch. Something she couldn't give up on, even if he'd only left her notes this morning.

The baby moved inside of her, as if he or she agreed with everything. Holly took that as a sign. It was better than listening to her fears.

"I'm ready for anything," Holly finally said.

"All right then." Rose sounded relieved, but Holly didn't know if that was for the campaign's sake or Holly's. "You call me if you need anything, okay? The campaign's important, but..."

The manager left it hanging. It was obvious that Rose had invested all her faith in Bo, too.

"Thank you, Rose," Holly said.

She hung up the phone, staring at it for what seemed like ages. Long enough so that, when she felt a twinge in her lower back, she snapped out of it.

Drawing in a breath between her teeth, Holly went to the bathroom, but when a wave of nausea rolled her, she got to her knees, leaning on the tub's ledge.

What was going on? This had never happened before...she'd never gotten sick...

After the ill feeling faded, Holly's common sense kicked in. She got her cell phone and laid down on the bedroom floor on her left side—she remembered having read somewhere that this was what to do in case of premature labor...which was *not* what was happening now, she told herself.

Then she waited for a time, seeing if she had reason to call the doctor. But after about a half hour, she was fine, and she crawled back into bed.

The dull ache of her back lessened, and she ran her hands over her belly, turning to the one person who would never make her wonder. Who would never leave notes or leave her hanging.

"No matter what," she told the baby, "we're going to make it. We don't have to count on anyone but ourselves."

And that included Bo.

Chapter Ten

The minute Bo pulled into a spot near the main entrance of the Thunder Canyon Resort, Rose stealthily opened the back door of the SUV and slipped inside quite naturally, as if she performed these kinds of spy-like maneuvers every day.

"Just so you know, I called to check in with Holly this morning," she said, tapping her cell phone against her palm while lasering that campaign manager/schoolmarm stare on him.

Bo surveyed her in the rearview mirror, wondering if he'd heard her correctly.

"Did you just say that you called my wife?" he asked.

"Yes, I did."

They were fifteen minutes early for a meeting, where they would be having a lunch with several local businessmen in the upscale Gallatin Room. He was going to listen to their suggestions and expectations for a new mayor, and he didn't have time for this—Rose inserting herself into his marriage.

He wasn't sure just why it seemed like such an invasion. It had to be those morning-after jitters he'd been experiencing.

Withdrawal from all his years of bachelorhood?

But he'd never gone through this kind of mental crisis before. Why now?

Why with Holly?

Rose held up her phone. "Contrary to what you might think, being your manager covers more than just politics, and I'll be doggoned if I leave damage behind me when I go back to huddling in my little house by the lake after this campaign. Based on what I saw between you and Holly last night, I suspect that communication with her is lacking, dear boy, so, yes, I took the initiative. I called her."

The warmth from the heater was cooling since Bo had shut down the engine, and it left the air with a gathering chill.

He took his gaze off the mirror and tugged on his leather gloves.

He wasn't going to ask what Holly had said during that phone call. But had she spilled her sorrows about Bo? Had his "wife" mentioned how he'd given into her last night and now he was acting like he regretted his folly so much that, this morning, he'd left polite, distant notes along with a breakfast?

Bo couldn't say how many times he'd almost gone back into Holly's room before he'd finally deserted the house for the office. He just knew that, every time, he'd held to the fact that being near Holly again would spell trouble.

Hell, once, his dad had probably brought his mom breakfast in bed. They had probably enjoyed mornings where they'd laughed together, lazing away a few hours until dragging themselves up and out, enjoying each other's company until…

Bo grabbed his hat from the passenger's seat. His parents had liked each other's company until something had happened to make them not like it. Who knew what the catalyst for their eventual separation had been—a single, decisive moment when they'd both decided that they didn't love each other? Or a string of circumstances that had built and built over the years, crushing them both under its weight until they couldn't take it anymore?

Whatever it was, Bo had promised that he would never repeat their mistakes, and that started with his unwillingness not to give up his heart—especially to someone who'd agreed to be only a temporary wife.

Yeah, this whole marriage hadn't gone how he'd anticipated, but he was determined to give his wife everything else she needed. He *wouldn't* be another Alan for Holly and her child, getting in too deep and then leaving, as most people seemed to do these days, whether it was through splitting up a marriage or even dying, as Holly's mom had done to Hank Pritchett.

Unlike the others, Bo was going to stay with Holly through thick and thin, supporting her even after their marriage ended. They'd just taken a wrong step last night, that's all, but he was going to fix that error, make her see that she was still highly valued, although they wouldn't go to bed again.

He wouldn't be leaving her at all. The kind of support

he was offering was stronger than love, which could disappear so quickly and easily.

Putting the hat on his head, Bo felt covered. "Well then, Rose. Seems as if your job description as campaign manager has a wide purview these days."

"Bo," Rose said.

There was a caring ring to her voice that made him stop reaching for the handle of the door.

Then she added, "I made your housekeeping my business because I see a train wreck coming, and I just can't sit by and watch it happen."

He almost told her to mind her own affairs, but then he looked into that rearview mirror again, saw the sympathy in her gaze.

He couldn't fool her, not Rose, who saw through so much.

Still, he pulled down his hat so it covered most of his eyes."For the first time in my life, I have no idea what to do. Can you believe that? Me, the man who wants to run Thunder Canyon."

A moment passed, as if Rose was surprised that he'd admitted it, and he heard himself going on, although he wasn't about to tell her everything about Holly.

About how involved they'd gotten last night.

"Holly and I have become…closer…than we thought we'd be," he said.

"I understand."

Did she?

"What did Holly say to you this morning?" he asked, giving in.

Rose glanced at the phone in her hand. "Nothing much, but that girl sure as heck isn't about to abandon ship. My impression, though, is that she's staying because of something other than the deal you made with her."

A thrust of fear jarred Bo.

Or was it something else so foreign that he just couldn't identify it?

Whatever the case, it remained in him, making him feel as if he was about to jump off a city skyscraper with nothing but a thin rope around his ankles.

"I won't go into details," he said, watching the windshield, how it was fogging, making the situation even hazier. "But I acted pretty wrongheaded before I left the house this morning. Like you said, I don't communicate very well with Holly. I'm not used to having to communicate with anyone."

"You're a well-entrenched bachelor, that's why. Did it ever occur to you, though, that you might learn how to function with a woman around?"

No, he thought. He'd learned a lot of lessons through observation, and it was too late for him. A bachelor always had a "good until" date on him before he went beyond the point of being good for anyone, and he'd reached it years ago.

So why was that strange feeling still floating around in him, as if waiting for him to claim it?

Rose clucked her tongue. "This is my fault, too. I shouldn't have been so cavalier about this plan, either."

"Now don't go saying stuff like that." He'd fisted his coat, which he'd pulled onto his lap. "I was the one who suggested it. I was the first to think it'd be fine and dandy to take advantage of a girl who was too young to know any better and in a bad position to boot."

"A *girl?*" Rose moved forward in the backseat. "Bo,

maybe you should take another look at Holly. She's no little girl. And I think she knows damned well what she wants out of life, even though she only needed a short time to get herself back on track after her experience with her ex."

Not a little girl.

And last night, Holly had made it clear that she wanted *him*. He'd returned each kiss, too. Damn it, even now he craved her, and it was more than he'd ever craved any woman.

But it wasn't fair to Holly—she'd come to care for a husband who couldn't return what she had to give. Bo just didn't have it in him, not beyond taking care of her and Hopper with money. He wasn't capable of…

There came that floating word again, but this time, Bo banged straight into it.

Love?

He tried to get away from it as fast as he could, but it stayed with him like a growing shadow, following his every dodge, refusing to go away.

He put on his coat, adding layers to himself.

"So that's it?" Rose asked. "That's where you're leaving this?"

"There's nowhere else for me to go." He put his hand on the door. "I was attempting to be the hero for Thunder Canyon, but I'm the bad guy. What else is there to say?"

"That you really did have her happiness in mind when you set out to do this?"

He had, but he could imagine Holly at home right now—how she probably wasn't smiling much. He hadn't made her life better at all, although that was what he promised everyone else in his rally speeches.

"I did want to make her happy," he said.

Rose laid a hand on his shoulder. When he glanced down at her fingers, he saw her old wedding ring, how the gold still glistened even years after her husband's death.

Just another case of being left behind, he thought, before realizing that Rose loved her husband enough to still wear that band.

"It looks like her happiness isn't the only thing that's being destroyed," Rose said.

It took Bo a second to comprehend what she was talking about.

His own happiness?

And maybe she was right. Holly was the best thing that had ever happened to him.

And the worst.

So what was left to do? Prolong their relationship and get in even deeper before it ultimately ended?

Hardly. But he had a different responsibility to Holly and the baby, and he was going to live up to it. He would just have to stay away from her in the carnal sense. No more bed play. No more kisses, caresses…

Slipping out from under Rose's hand on his shoulder, he opened the car door and went outside, feeling as if he had muddled through some small part of his dilemma.

At least until he got home tonight.

After the business lunch, Bo had decided to call Holly, just to keep tabs on her. It was the right thing to do, he told himself.

The good guy thing.

But their conversation had been brief, to the point

and all business, so when they hung up, he didn't feel any better.

For the rest of the day, the air pressed down on him like a slab of granite slowly falling from the sky, and he couldn't get out from under it while he checked in with the foremen from his ranches, who had taken over operations when Bo had decided to run for office. Things didn't improve while he performed door-to-door campaign visits, either.

He just couldn't erase Holly from his mind.

Bo finally got home around dinnertime, arriving to the aroma of cabbage, beef and bread. When he discovered Holly in front of the kitchen stove, a wooden spoon in one hand as she stirred the contents of a cast-iron pan, he couldn't concentrate on anything but the curls that had escaped from the barrette holding her hair away from her face, how they tickled the smooth skin of her neck.

Skin he'd taken so much joy in kissing last night.

Bo didn't know what had filled his veins, but it didn't feel like blood anymore—it felt more like fluid strings, pulling him closer to Holly, tightening his insides, wrapping him up in a helpless bundle.

Then he noticed that she had her other hand on her back, as if it was aching.

He started to ask what was wrong, but she must've sensed him standing there and she turned around.

There was no pain on her face, just a smile—a glimpse of sunshine—that blinded him. Or maybe blindsided would've been a better word.

But then she seemed to remember that he'd left her notes this morning, and her expression cooled.

"Hi," she said. "How was the rest of your day?"

The alteration in her mood affected him, his gut smarting, as if pummeled.

"Good." Then he gestured toward her back. All business—he would remember that and not expect any more smiles that he didn't deserve. "Is your back okay?"

"Oh." She looked down at her hand, as if she hadn't realized she'd propped it in such a position. "Yeah, I'm fine. I had a bit of an ache here this morning, a little nausea, too, but my time's approaching and my body's going to be adjusting. It's not a big deal."

"So everything's normal?"

"You don't really want to hear about the details of pregnancy, Bo."

"Yes, Holly, I do."

He'd said it before censoring himself, but, hell, he wasn't sorry. Not even when she got a surprised look on her face.

Did she really believe that he didn't give a crap… even if they were just faux spouses?

"Whether you want to talk or not," he said, "you deserve a sit. I've got the rest of dinner."

She turned off a burner, and he led her to a kitchen chair.

"The food's almost done," she said.

"Then that'll make this all the easier on me."

She leaned back in her seat, and he pulled over another chair so she could prop her feet on it. She was wearing thick pink woolen socks under her long flannel skirt and he remembered how cute her toes had been, how graceful the arches of her feet were while he'd massaged them last night.

Holly smiled at him in thanks, and that did even more to slay Bo.

"Did you call the doctor about those aches from this morning?" he asked almost gruffly, going to the stove. After stirring the beef and bean sprouts dish, he extinguished that burner, then moved to the oven, which showed that the wheat bread had only about thirty seconds left on the timer, so he turned off the heat there, as well.

Turned off the heat *everywhere.*

"I didn't need to call her, Bo. But just to make you feel better, if the aches persist, I'll go in for an appointment."

Guilt was niggling at him. Backaches. Nausea.

Had their activities last night done something to the baby?

He would never forgive himself if that was true.

He knew what he had to do now. The right thing. The only thing.

"Holly," he said, sitting down at the table with her. "I'm worried about the baby's safety."

She nodded, as if wondering where he was going with this, although he suspected she knew, based on the wary shadows that had crept into her gaze.

"And," he said, "I think it might be wise for us to back off of the physical stuff between us."

There. A firm excuse to stay away from her. A down payment on buying more time for this marriage, because if they didn't have to deal anymore with the tension sex presented, they would get along a whole lot better.

But Bo didn't feel so great when Holly visibly straightened in her chair, her shoulders stiffening. She even blinked, as if belatedly absorbing a mental blow.

Bo didn't know if he could hate anyone more than he did himself at this moment.

"What I mean," he said, trying to soften the situation, "is that this backache and nausea from this morning might be directly tied to physical activity."

"Dr. Aberline said that I could be careful on the... honeymoon." She glanced at the table. "That sex is okay as long as it isn't too strenuous. She said that I might not be too in the mood for making love, anyway, but..."

But he knew from reading that some women's hormones revved up.

And *he* did that to Holly.

"You're going into your eighth month," he said in a last ditch effort. "We should be as careful as possible."

She kept her head lowered, but she nodded again.

His relief at her agreement didn't wipe away that self-disgust that had taken root in him, the feeling that they hadn't solved anything between them.

He rose from his chair, intending to prepare the rest of dinner, but then she spoke.

"Bo? I wanted to ask you. This morning...The notes..."

He didn't move.

"I'm..." She set both of her hands on the table, as if to prime herself. "I'm wondering if last night meant anything to you."

Crash.

Too late to run, because that weight that had been pressing down on him all day had fallen, pinning him.

"It's just," she continued, "that I woke up this morning and you were gone."

When she finally met his gaze, her eyes were such a sad blue that Bo wanted to reassure her, tell her that he was still here, even if she couldn't have all of him.

But he kept his distance. It was an act of pure will, a

point of survival, because if he touched her, he would never come back from it.

In the back of his mind, he saw his mom and dad sitting at this same dinner table, a chasm between them even though they were only a few feet apart as they ate in silence after realizing that they shouldn't have gotten married in the first place.

"Holly," Bo said, venturing all he could without stepping back over the line with her, "I hope you don't think I left because I regret last night. You're more than a man like me could've ever hoped for."

When Bo realized that his words echoed those he'd said to the heckler at the campaign rally, he left the room, unable to bear the look he knew he would see on her face.

As well as the expression he was afraid *she* would see on his.

The next days teemed with so many items on Holly's to-do lists that she and Bo barely saw each other.

Then again, maybe that was for the best. From the talk she'd had with Bo on the night after they'd made love, she didn't have a heck of a lot of optimism about where their marriage stood.

She had come on strong to him, thinking that he'd wanted sex just as much as she did, and he hadn't been cruel enough to tell her the truth about why he wouldn't go to bed with her again. Instead, he'd conjured up that "no sex because of the baby" excuse. She was sure of it. He was doing everything he could not to come straight out and say what he really meant: that he didn't do long-term. That she wasn't really even his type, except that she had forced the issue between them, and what man could resist such a willing woman?

But she was a woman who was in control. And even if she couldn't figure out how her feelings fit into the big picture with Bo, she would live.

She would deal.

Yet, much to her dismay, her growing feelings for him wouldn't die, and she kept thinking that maybe, after the election, their relationship would have the room to breathe a little, to clarify itself. But the election seemed like such a long way off, even though it was only a few days away.

At any rate, before the big day came, she would have to get through the rest of the campaigning—tonight in particular.

The Halloween fund-raiser for Bo's cause.

The last big hurrah.

It arrived just as quickly as every night seemed to, and as Holly stood in the midst of Thunder Canyon Resort's grand lobby, she slowed down by pouring herself a plastic glass of orange punch at the buffet table, then taking a good look around.

The big elk sculpture had been decorated with little floating ghosties, the fireplace hung with sprawling black spider webs. A DJ had been hired to play songs like "Monster Mash," and everyone who supported Bo had arrived in full costume.

Near the foot of the stairway, Erika waved to Holly from amongst a group of other women. Her friend had dressed as a lace-mantilla-wearing senorita, which went along well with her fiancé's Zorro costume. Dillon was off somewhere else at the moment though, not that Erika seemed to mind as she chatted with Tori Jones, with her free-spirited gypsy costume, and Haley Anderson, who had seized the opportunity to play a vampiress for the night. Somewhere around here, both women's costumed significant others were in full garb, too: Connor McFarlane, the reluctant, leather-coated gypsy man, and Marlon Cates, Van Helsing to Haley's vamp.

Holly further scanned the crowd, finding Grant and Steph Clifton—Buffalo Bill and Calamity Jane—nearby, but she didn't see the person she was really looking for.

Just as the world got a bit less interesting, she discovered her husband emerging from a crowd of young supporters, his very presence spiking the energy level in the room.

And in Holly.

He was dressed in a Prince Charles uniform—in the dark, blue-sashed, gold-braided, ribbon-medaled suit the royal had worn during his wedding to Diana—and he was…dashing.

So handsome, so cowboy noble in all his regalia, even while still wearing that darned Stetson.

It felt as if Holly's heart was shrinking and expanding all at the same time. But how was that possible? How could she be punctured yet still so in love?

She set down her punch on the table before it slipped from her hand. All she needed was to ruin her Princess Di wedding gown. Ruin the night altogether.

Rose, who'd decided that *she* would make a grand Queen Elizabeth II in her crown, sash and royal dress, came to the buffet table, standing next to Holly with a plate of buffalo wings and an orange frosted cupcake.

"You look lonely over here."

"Lonely in a crowd? How can that be?" Holly said it lightly, but the meaning hung heavily in the air.

The other woman smiled at her. Rose had been doing that a lot lately, especially once the Charles and Di costumes had been delivered. She had ordered them just after Bo and Holly's own wedding, looking far ahead to the Halloween fund-raiser with the idea of carrying through with the whole Windsor fairy tale romance theme that the press had created. The other day, Rose had even offered to replace these Charles and Di costumes, but Holly had declined.

She would deal.

As she swallowed away a lump in her throat, she added, *I should admit to a work of fiction when I'm in one.*

The sooner she accepted that a constructed story was all her relationship with Bo would ever be, the better, right? But then she would remember what Bo had said to her when he had been on his knees, just before they made love, with his hands cupping her stomach.

You're everything I could ever imagine.

With all her heart, she believed that he had meant it, but the more days that went by, the more she knew that Bo wasn't the same man he'd been that night. In the long run, he wasn't built to be that guy, and he'd told her as much before she'd ever led him to her bed. He'd said he wasn't the marrying type, and she should've listened. She just hadn't wanted to.

Rose was obviously intent on taking Holly's mind off of anything heavy, thank goodness, and she gestured to a single man who was lingering near the lobby's entrance. He was costumed in a Lone Ranger outfit, complete with a half-mask, holsters and red kerchief. Strands of silver hair peeked out from under his white hat.

Holly would recognize him anywhere. "Are you kidding? Is that Arthur Swinton?"

Rose had trouble holding back a chuckle.

"Good heavens," Holly said. "He's subtle, isn't he? Or was he invited through some sort of ridiculous error?"

"Not invited. My guess is that he's slinking around to gauge the crowd and the amount of support they're throwing behind Bo. And from that frown, I'm going to say Swinton's worried about the momentum Bo seems to have gained lately. I'll be keeping my eye on him as long as he's here."

When Bo's voice interrupted, Holly realized that Rose had distracted her well enough so that she hadn't seen him crossing the room.

"Keeping your eye on who, Rose?"

Holly's pulse gave a mighty yank.

"Swinton," Rose said.

Bo subtly followed the direction of his manager's nod, and when he saw Swinton, he grinned. Then he reached over Holly, brushing against her puffed bridal sleeve as he went for a cup of punch.

She smelled him—musk, soap—and the night they'd been together came crashing back to her, a wave of drowning remembrance.

It seemed as if he felt it, too, because he hauled in a long breath, then stood away from her.

A safe distance, she thought. Their modus operandi.

Rosc said, "Swinton's not our only mystery guest tonight."

"Who else crashed our party?" Bo asked.

Rose gestured toward the stairway, where a few couples loitered near the top—Matt Cates dressed in Paul Bunyan flannels and accompanied by his occasional girlfriend Christine Mayhew, who'd taken the sexy route and assumed the guise of a svelte kitty cat. Next to them, a lone woman took her time descending the steps. A woman in a feathered mask, dressed all in white, like a swan.

"Erin Castro," Rose said. "But she was invited."

Bo frowned. "I thought she didn't want anything to do with my campaign."

Rose had approached her about doing a PR spot for Bo, one in which she could give a testimonial about what made Thunder Canyon great, why she'd moved here and decided to stay.

"You're right, Erin declined any part of our PR," Rose said. "I get the feeling she's skittish about revealing much about herself."

"Well, you read people pretty well, so I wouldn't doubt it," Bo said.

Holly wasn't too bad at reading, either, and the palpable tension that stood between her and Bo made her think that he just as aware of her as she was of him.

Just as needful…

Rose planted her long-gloved hands on her hips. "Erin's interesting to read. She asked a few questions about you and the other Cliftons, Bo, and I couldn't help thinking her interest was somehow…noteworthy."

"What do you mean?"

"I can't say what it was exactly. But there's something about Erin Castro…"

She stopped talking, smiling instead, and Holly knew that it was because someone was approaching.

The Lone Ranger, Arthur Swinton.

The older man tipped his hat to Holly, then to Rose. He did no such thing for Bo.

"Quite a party," he said. "Then again, Bo, I'm sure you're well versed in throwing decadent shindigs."

"I'm adept at a good many things, Arthur, one of which is going to be leading Thunder Canyon out of the muck."

"We'll see about that."

Although Swinton was smiling below his half-mask, Holly detected anxiety around the lines of his mouth.

With that, he made his way through the crowd, toward the door.

Bo watched him go, and Rose tweaked his sleeve.

"He came over just to see if he could rattle you," she said. "We've got him."

"It's not over 'til it's over."

As if some kind of social dam had been broken, a reporter, who, like the other members of the press here, hadn't dressed up, came over with his camera. He held it up, just as Rose followed in Swinton's wake, probably to see that he made it out of the party without causing any kind of ruckus.

"How about some photos of the royal couple?" the journalist asked.

"Of course," Bo said.

Holly put on her best wife smile. It felt so out of place, even if she'd gotten so proficient at it.

Yet the second Bo nestled his arm around her, it was the real thing—a flow of silent sighs that infused her, making her weak.

When Bo smiled down at her, she bit her lower lip to keep it from shaking. And when she thought she saw something in his gaze—a darker shade of blue, a flicker of confusion that she was feeling, too—Holly unthinkingly rested her arms around his waist.

For a series of flashes, she believed that Bo might even kiss her, here, now, in spite of his determination not to have any more physical play.

His lips parted, as if he was imagining the night they'd been together, and she tilted her chin, raising herself to him, ready, hoping…

"Bo," said a reporter, cracking open the moment and snagging Bo's gaze away from her. "How's marriage for the former bachelor?"

Holly swallowed, a flush consuming her.

Had anyone noticed what she'd revealed?

A crowd had gathered near them, as if drawn by the fantasy of their romance. Townspeople she'd grown up with, their hands cupped over their hearts, smiling at how life had turned out for the girl they'd seen mature.

Funny, Holly thought. At home, there was a moratorium on romance between her and Bo, but here, in front of everyone, they were a romantic dream come true, just like Charles and Di. All glamour on the outside, all sadness underneath.

Bo turned on the charm for the crowd. "Marriage?"

He glanced down at Holly, and there was that look again—the gentleness, the…

She wouldn't think it was love, not like she'd made the mistake of doing with Alan.

Bo's gaze grew serious as he completed his thought to the public. "If I'd known marriage would be like this, I would've done it much sooner."

Everyone laughed as more bulbs tried to shed light on them.

"But," Bo added, resting his fingers on Holly's cheek, his touch burning, "I suppose I had to wait for my wife to come to her senses and have me. The wait sure was worth it though. Believe me."

His gaze devoured her, and Holly gave him everything back in her own look.

Anything you want, Bo. I'd give you that and more if you'd only have me.

"Bo!" another reporter shouted. "Have you checked in with the news in the last fifteen minutes? According to a poll conducted by your town paper, you're the front-runner! What do you think of that?"

A cheer—and it wasn't just from the crowd. It welled up in Holly, too.

When Bo scooped her into an impulsive hug, she knew it was really him doing it, not her supposed husband.

She hugged him back, whispering in his ear, "Congratulations."

He palmed the back of her head, careful of her full Princess Di veil, careful of the baby, whose bump skimmed him.

So real…

All too soon, other reporters were lobbing questions at Bo, and he had to speak loudly to answer.

"Here's the reason for my success!" he said, smiling at Holly. "A good woman by the side of every man!"

She wanted to believe in that, but every stab of a flash was like a knife to her heart, and she wondered just how much of these lies she could take before she bled out altogether.

Chapter Eleven

On election day, Bo stood, too agitated to sit, while he stared at his private office windows in campaign headquarters. He'd closed the blinds for isolation as he listened to the local radio station, awaiting word of the final vote count, which would come at any time now.

He wished Holly was in here with him. She had only gone to get coffee from the main area outside, where his volunteers were listening to the broadcast, too, but Bo didn't want to hear the results without her, maybe because they had become such a team. Because they had worked so hard to get here. Because…

He flailed for a better answer as a soft knock rattled the door.

When Holly came inside, holding a cup of coffee for him, the sound of the droning radio seemed to disappear into the back of Bo's head.

It happened every time he saw her—the world, falling away in layers to reveal his wife at the center.

But, as always, he bound everything right back up and, instead, smiled at her in thanks as she handed over the beverage.

She returned his smile, and he thought of how she looked like a real politician's wife tonight, in a cranberry suit with a faux-fur collar. The material swaddled her bump, and Bo wouldn't be surprised if the press celebrated her taste in chic baby suits by plastering more starry-eyed pictures of him and her across the media landscape.

Western Royals, they'd taken to calling the Bo Cliftons. A fairy-tale happily ever after. Why just look at how the two of them gazed at each other, touched each other…

"Don't be nervous," Holly said.

"I'm not."

He drank some of the coffee. Strong and black… she knew how he preferred it. She'd come to know a lot about him except for the most important parts—the ones he wished he could share with her.

But he knew what was best for him…for them…in the long run, and it wasn't him trying in vain to be a husband or dad.

"You're totally nervous," she said matter-of-factly.

"Maybe a little." He grinned. "It's not over 'til it's over."

Holly laughed. "Rose and I have told you a million times—all the early polls say you've got it in the bag. You've heard it on the radio, too."

"I try not to count my chickens before they hatch,

though I don't mind rushing the hatching along. You know me that well, Holly."

His last words were like a specter that had hung around after Halloween.

You know me...

Her eyes had gotten that melancholy cast to them again, as if she was remembering that they didn't really know each other at all and he was doing his best to make sure of it.

Just as his heart started to drag him down, his cell phone rang.

He and Holly glanced at each other before he answered it. She watched him, her hand over her mouth, her eyes wide.

"Hello?"

"Congratulations," a stern voice said. "It's yours."

Swinton.

When Bo smiled at Holly, she got the gist of the call, and she beamed, sending bolts of jubilation into him, too.

"You ran an energetic race, Arthur," Bo said. He'd told himself that he wouldn't mention Swinton's mudslinging. He'd act with the dignity Thunder Canyon needed.

"I'm about to make my concession speech, but before I step out there, I just have one thing to say."

Bo let him have his moment.

Swinton's voice lowered. "I'll still be around, Clifton, and I'll be keeping an eye on you."

"Thank you, Arthur. Have a great night."

Bo hung up, not dwelling on what Swinton might have meant. Was he talking about his marriage or his mayoral policies in general?

Not that it mattered, as Holly waited for him to say something.

Now that Swinton was off the phone, the news was sinking in, still partly a dream.

But Holly...She wasn't a figment of his imagination.

Without stopping to think, Bo rushed to her, taking her in his arms, mindful of the baby, even while embracing her.

She was laughing wildly as he buried his face in her curls.

"We did it!" he said against her ear.

Holly's laughter ended on a gasp, and it was as if they both just realized that their bodies were close, intimate in this moment of triumph.

He even thought he could feel her heart pounding, through the atmosphere, into him, just like that night they'd fallen into bed.

The night he'd replayed over and over again in his mind.

They drew back from each other, her curls falling away from the stubble on his cheek, a few still clinging to the five o'clock shadow. And, as they stared into one another's eyes, he yearned to put his arms around her again, ask her to stay in his life, because he never wanted this to be over.

But that had to be the euphoria of the moment, right?

That's all it was...

The announcement came over the radio, but it was only background as Bo and Holly stayed locked in the bubble of this victory. Of what they were to each other.

"It's official," the reporter said. "We just received news that Arthur Swinton has conceded. Bo Clifton is our new mayor by a landslide!"

When the door burst open, that bubble burst, and it was as if the surroundings popped, too, everything going back into fast motion, loud and insane.

Rose was cheering, and so were the volunteers who spilled into Bo's office behind her. They hugged Holly and, in the chaos, they swept Bo farther and farther away from her, out the door, shoving his coat and hat at him as they pushed him into the cold night air until he got to the town square, where a bunch of townsfolk had gathered at a podium draped with red-white-and-blue.

Surreal, the people waiting for him out there, drowning out his thoughts with their voices, their yells of hope.

All the while, Bo looked for Holly.

Because nothing meant much without her to celebrate it with him.

Someone had turned on a microphone, and the glare of flashbulbs and news camera lights from stations in Bozeman and Billings, who'd decided that Bo's "mythology" was noteworthy stuff, distracted him. He saw his friends at the front of the crowd: Grant and Steph, so proud of their cousin. The Cates brothers, along with Haley Anderson.

Bo was just focusing on Dillon and Erika when he saw Erika's face light up even more as she spotted someone to her left.

Holly, and she was being escorted to his side by Rose.

His manager took Holly's hand, giving his wife over to him, and...

It was almost as if Bo was taking Holly and the baby into his life again during a second wedding.

But he couldn't think about that now. Everything was speeding by, leaving his lungs shallow.

Even as the cameras flashed and the crowd chanted—"Gold with Bo! Gold with Bo!"—Holly's hand slowly slipped out of his, gone.

Just as she soon would be, now that the election was over.

Back at the house, after a night of celebrating in the campaign office, Holly slumped onto the sofa in the living room while Bo, as usual, headed for a separate room.

Even after tonight's victory, he'd left her alone.

She pressed a hand over her eyes, hoping it would help to discourage tears of exhaustion, happiness… despair.

It'd been a long night, a long few weeks, and she was done, even before the inauguration.

And she didn't just mean she was done with Bo's political career, either. She couldn't continue with this roller coaster—Bo looking like he really did love her one minute, then coming back here and turning into a stranger the next.

Did he even have any idea of what had passed between them yet *again,* after he'd won? The moment when he'd taken her in his arms, as if she was the only person he wanted to cheer with? The emotion that had been so obvious to her when she'd come to him at the podium, before he'd given a rousing acceptance speech to Thunder Canyon?

No, she was sure he didn't have any clue, because he'd

gotten what he wanted tonight, and it had very little to do with her.

Bo entered the living room, standing by the edge of the sofa, the mayor of Thunder Canyon in his boots, blue jeans and Western shirt. A man who still made her want to cry every time she even thought about him.

"Looks like you didn't quite make it to your room," he said.

"I wasn't heading there just yet." She was so tired that she *wasn't* tired. But maybe that was because her soul wasn't giving her any peace.

"Well," he said, and his comment didn't head anywhere else.

She looked up, and she could see the reaction she caused in him—that softening of his blue eyes. Then the way he seemed to fortify himself afterward.

He laughed, and it wasn't a comfortable sound. "Married less than a month and here we are, already out of conversation."

Just listen to that. Holly would've said that he had given up on their marriage a long time ago, but she knew that he'd never really *started* with it. To him, relationships didn't exist but for a string of dates or an arranged union.

Done...I'm so...

She sighed, and it hurt.

...done.

"Bo, what conversation would we be having right now if you had lost the election?"

"I didn't lose."

He had no idea what was about to hit him. "Could you just be honest with me? I'm a big girl. I can take it."

He gave her a look that was so filled with respect

and—yes—adoration that a tiny burst of hope roared to life in her.

"I know you're a big girl," he said. "Rose keeps saying that, and I've known it for a while now."

"And?"

He raised his hands halfway, as if showing her that they were empty. "Six months, Holly. That's what we said."

"You're telling me that, if you had lost tonight, you still would've kept me around, even though I didn't have any more use to you politically."

"Right." He said it as if he was pulling it out from his core, as if he couldn't believe that she didn't already know how he would answer. "I…"

Say it, Bo, she thought. *All you have to do is say it.*

But he didn't.

Holly closed her eyes. When a tear leaked out—damn it—she wiped it away, hoping he hadn't seen.

He got down to his knees next to her, whisking his fingertips along the damp trail that the tear had left.

His voice was thick. "I never meant to make you cry. I should've known I would."

"Stop it." She opened her eyes. "Stop being so gloom and doom about marriage. I know we didn't get together for the right reasons, but just for future reference, has it ever occurred to you that you do more sabotaging than a marriage could ever do to itself? That you make sure that you fail at it before it can fail you?"

"Yes, I've thought of that."

She had to wait a moment for that to make sense to her. He knew? He just didn't *want* to stop himself?

Oh, God, she and the baby meant less to him than she'd ever thought. She'd been imagining everything.

He'd only decided to be nice to her, to let her down easily after he'd seen that she was taking this marriage too seriously—she'd been right about that.

In her mind's eye, she saw Alan walking out the door again. She'd imagined that he'd been attached to her, and she'd dumbly repeated the mistake with Bo.

And it *was* so much more agonizing now.

"I see," she said, wishing she could just disappear off the face of the earth.

"The last thing I ever wanted to do was be another Alan for you, Holly."

"You're not." Couldn't he see that? She hadn't loved Alan as she loved Bo, and she didn't think she could ever feel this way about anyone again.

"I just thought there'd be no complications in our arrangements," he said, "no…"

She wanted to hear him say it. "What?"

When he didn't speak, she rallied. If she was imagining what Bo felt for her and the baby, she wanted irrefutable proof. She would let go if she had it.

Only then.

"You didn't think there'd be any love between us?" she said.

He started to stand, but she reached out and pulled him back down.

"I'm putting my heart on the line here, Bo. At least do me the favor of telling me yes or no."

"And what good would it do?"

The tears were rushing her again, but Holly couldn't hold them back. "You can't even say that there's hope for something with us?"

His shoulders slumped, and with a pain in his gaze

that she couldn't reach, he rested both hands on her belly.

"Isn't it enough," he said, "to tell you that even after six months is up, you can stay here as long as you want? That I've grown to like having you and Hopper around and that you'll always have a home here?"

The flicker of hope in her burned a little higher now. He was getting closer to admitting what she knew was in him.

As Bo kept his hands on her belly, she bent to him, resting her lips on the top of his head. His thick hair felt so silky, and she slid her fingers through it, easing her other arm around his back until his face was nestled against her neck. The skin there tingled, sending a wash of sparks through her.

If she kissed him, would he see more clearly?

If she showed him how much love she could give him…?

Holly pressed her lips against his head, then his temple, his cheek.

"I don't want to go anywhere after this deal has been played out," she whispered. "But I need a reason to stay."

Then she kissed his lips, and just like that first night, when they'd loved each other, he responded.

Soft. She'd never known a man could have such soft lips.

She reclined on the sofa, taking him with her, kissing him with such agonizing slowness that she didn't think she would survive past this moment.

"Be my husband," she said, leading one of his hands to the buttons on her suit. "Tell me that you want us to stay because of a better reason than you just like having us around."

His hand splayed over her breast, and she gasped, his mere touch enough to send spikes of passion through her.

He lowered his head, as if fighting himself. "I don't make promises like that. You don't want me to, because you'll find yourself sorely disappointed in the end."

"You won't disappoint. I believe that, Bo, just as much as I believed in your becoming mayor."

She undid one of the large buttons on her top, another. Then she unsnapped the front hook of her bra, guiding his hand inside. As soon as his flesh met hers, she winced in pure pleasure.

His fingers skimmed her nipple, and she bit her lip as a buzz started to hum between her legs.

She wanted a real honeymoon with him.

If she had a reason to stay.

If he would just say it.

"Tell me," she said. "Tell me there's hope."

He paused, and silently, she urged him on.

But when he withdrew his hand from inside her top, taking care to close it before he leaned away from her, she remembered how it had felt when she had sat in the middle of the room, pregnant and afraid, hours after Alan had gone.

The same rejection, all over again.

The same failure that she'd been so afraid to admit to.

But she had to now, because she'd lost again, and it was more than she could stand. Even in her giddiest moments with Alan, she'd never felt like this—as if every second of her life was enhanced when Bo was around, as if he was the first and last person she wanted to see when the day started and ended.

If a heart could actually break, Holly's was doing it.

Slowly, mustering all the dignity she could manage, she buttoned her top, then took off the ring he had given her.

When she held it out to him, Bo sat back on his heels. "Don't do this, Holly."

She leaned forward and dropped the ring into the opening of his shirt pocket, her body shaking with the emotion she had to hold in, because she wouldn't let him see her sob.

Her back had started aching, but she hadn't noticed when it'd started. Maybe it was the stress, but she didn't let that stop her from what she had to do.

"Now that you're the mayor, I'm going to leave," she said. "I promised I'd stay until spring, but I can't take this anymore." A near sob pushed her next comment out. "I just love you too much to be around you, Bo."

As her statement reverberated through him, he stood, watching as the tears gathered in her eyes again.

Those big blue eyes that comforted him, that invited him to go places he'd never thought possible before.

Love. She loved him.

And she was leaving.

If Bo could just tell her what she wanted to hear, she would improve him. It should be that easy, but years and years of seeing how good intentions got warped during marriage had left their mark, and Bo had never made a promise he couldn't deliver.

Yet she was *leaving,* and the reality of it just kept blasting away at him.

"Don't go," he finally said, but it hadn't come out in the persuasive way he'd intended.

Couldn't he just say that he'd begun to feel for her, too?

Holly was holding her hand to the small of her back, and he stepped toward her. Panic—the same as he'd experienced before when he thought the baby was in danger—mauled him.

"You've got another back pain."

"I'll be fine once I get out of here."

Stubborn. Damn, she was bullheaded.

But he could sure as hell be, too.

Without preamble, he bent down, scooped her into his arms, then carried her to her bedroom.

"What're you doing?" she asked, her voice tight.

"Putting you on your bed. Locking you in. Making sure you don't go anywhere and that you rest for now. Then I'm calling the doctor about these backaches."

"Don't worry about it," she said, repeating what he'd told her over and over this past month.

But he did worry. So much, too much.

He didn't say anything until he got to her bedroom and laid her on the mattress. Right away, his feisty wife sat up, getting off the bed and going for the closet, her hand still on her back. She pulled out a suitcase.

Damn it.

"Holly," he said.

"I've heard all I need to from you."

"What about the baby?"

That froze her surely enough. She sent him a furious

look. “Are you reminding me that I’m shortchanging my child by leaving you?”

Bo took a big breath, then let it out. “I’m telling you that it’s not an act when I touch your stomach. I picture Hopper in there, and…”

The line. Here it was, and he straddled it. It had to be enough to keep her here.

Wouldn’t it be?

“…it’s as if he or she is my very own child,” he finished. “I’d be proud to have your child known as my son or daughter. I’ve already come to love the little bugger.”

Holly hesitated over her open suitcase. Then she whispered, “I’ve noticed your affection…for the baby.”

But he couldn’t say the rest, committing himself to Holly, not just the baby. He couldn’t forget about the day he’d realized, even when he was about ten, that his mom and dad didn’t act like other married people. That they seemed to regret being with each other, though they’d validated that notion only years later, long after Bo had left the roost.

When he didn’t continue, Holly’s shoulders hunched. Her sadness broke him down.

He went to her, but she held up a hand.

Before she could tell him to stay away, she sucked in a breath, holding her stomach.

“Holly?”

She sank to her knees at the bedside, grasping the mattress. “I think I…”

“What?”

“Contraction…”

He didn’t get it at first. Then the terror came.

Too early… She was only eight months along…

Panic consumed Bo, and he took her into his arms again, carrying her out of her room, his heartbeat ramming his chest as she grabbed his shirt, fear filling her gaze.

He couldn't imagine a world without Hopper…without them both.

Dear God, he'd given her a hard time, and look what he'd done…

"It'll be okay," Bo said as he brought her to the SUV, sounding so put together, even though all he wanted to do was run with her to the truck then slam down on the gas pedal, burning rubber.

But the last thing she needed was a hysterical husband.

He got his wife to the hospital just after the next contraction hit.

Chapter Twelve

Hat clenched in his hand, Bo must've paced the tile in the empty Thunder Canyon General Hospital waiting room a thousand times over, but he wasn't keeping count.

Not when Holly and the baby were behind those swinging doors and he didn't know what the hell was happening with them.

Was his wife in pain? In labor?

And how about the baby…was it too early for him or her to be born?

Bo came to the doors, looking through the circular windows, but he only saw a sterile hallway with doctors walking around, clipboards in hand, stray wheelchairs lining the sides. It was a slow night here, and he suspected that Holly might be the center of attention back where a few of the doctors were heading, in a room that he couldn't see past where the hallway ended.

Damn it, Bo was never going to forgive himself if Holly and the baby came out of this for the worse. It was all his fault that they were even in here. He should've just given in to Holly, told her that he was going to change from the cynical bachelor into the man she needed.

That he loved her.

The air in his lungs felt so thin and sharp that he thought it might cut right through him.

Now that the threat of losing Holly and the baby was here, Bo couldn't lie to himself anymore.

They really were his everything.

Behind him, he heard the sliding hospital entrance doors open. When he glanced over his shoulder, Rose was there, running to him with open arms.

He'd called her as soon as the hospital staff had taken Holly behind those doors, leaving Bo stranded.

Rose must have seen how tortured he felt, because she pulled him in for a hug.

"How are they?" Rose asked.

"No progress reports yet."

She tightened her arms around him. "Holly's got a core of iron running through her, Bo."

"I know it." And he prayed it would be enough.

"I told you that I'd call her dad, so all the Pritchetts should be here soon, along with Erika and half of Thunder Canyon. I also called—"

Before she finished, the doors slid open again. His dad and mom walked in, circumventing the dull green waiting chairs.

Bo's father got to him first, the crags of his face

even deeper now, furrowed with concern as he pulled his son in for an embrace. Without a word, his mother gave Bo a remorseful attempt at a greeting smile right before she took up Bo's other side, cradling his head against her shoulder.

She was wearing a fashionable red cape-coat, no doubt a dramatic purchase from her Italy trip. Her blond hair was dyed to perfection and her nails manicured. After the divorce, she'd left behind the country girl, seeking bigger travels and adventures that the ranch had never afforded.

But she had on the same perfume Bo had been smelling since he was knee-tall. Jasmine. It brought him back to a time when they'd all been together. It drove home the fact that he had his *own* family now, and if Holly and the baby came out of this, he was going to fight to the death to save it.

Rose had already gone to the nurse's station, where a few Halloween decorations still remained. His manager was probably going to crack the whip to see if she could get better information.

Meanwhile, Bo's mom framed his face with her hands, getting a good gander at him. "You look like you're about to drop. Come sit with us."

"I can't sit."

His dad patted Bo's arm. "Of course not. And I told your mom…"

His father stopped himself, and Bo knew it was because he didn't want to start any arguments with his ex-wife. Even in Bo's fog of anguish, he saw how his parents still couldn't be around each other.

Wrinkling his brow, he finally got his mind in gear.

He *wouldn't* end up like them. There wouldn't ever

come a day when he'd want Holly out of his life. He was sure of it.

And he felt sorry for his parents because they'd never had the luxury of being so certain.

"I didn't realize you'd be in town, Mom," he said. "I thought you were coming for my inauguration. Dad, I thought you'd left after the wedding."

His dad cleared his throat. "Actually, we came to terms with our situation…for now. After a good phone discussion, we both decided to come to Thunder Canyon to be with you for the election results, but we didn't make up our minds soon enough to arrive on time. Then we got calls from Rose, and we just came straight here."

His mom tucked her hand into his. "I returned home from my trip yesterday, but I'd already decided that I was going to be here for you, since I made the wrong choice about attending your wedding. Forgive me, Bo?"

He looked at them—his parents. Two people standing apart, miles between them.

"It's okay, Mom," he said. He didn't have the energy to tell her he wished she and his dad had gotten it together earlier, because that's not what mattered now.

Holly and the baby were his everything, just as he'd believed that night when he'd gotten to his knees before he and his wife had made love. And he was going to prove it, if he had another opportunity with Holly.

Yes, there was going to be a change in Bo, even though it meant risk. Change had been easy to talk about in politics, but when it came to personal alterations, it was scarier than hell, and Bo had never been willing to chance it until Holly had come along.

A doctor emerged from the swinging doors, and Bo strode over to her, just as Rose came over from the nurse's station to join him and his parents.

The scrub-garbed doctor was smiling, and Bo nearly collapsed. There wouldn't be smiles if they were in dire straits, right?

"I'm Dr. Aberline, Holly's practitioner." Then she laid it out. "We stopped her labor. Holly and your baby are doing well—tired, but in good shape."

Holly and *his* baby.

Bo took hold of a chair to steady himself. He was shaking with relief, a well of emotion ready to burst out of him now that he knew they were okay.

Rose asked what he couldn't. "What was wrong?"

"There were some contractions, all right, but the baby needs more time to develop inside Holly. We gave her medication to relax the uterus. Holly's a healthy mother, yet I'm sure the stress of the election and a little dehydration did its part in this. Now that it's over, Mr. Mayor," she said, her smile growing as she glanced at Bo, "I hope you'll see to it that Holly gets plenty of rest and fluids."

"I'd bring the moon down from the sky for her."

Even as he said it, he realized that he'd always meant the romantic quotes he'd fed to the public and press about Holly and his family—that they had never, ever been an act.

With a start, he realized that change wasn't coming.

It had already arrived.

"Can I see her?" he asked.

"She's asleep, Mr. Clifton, but I can take you back there."

He left his hat behind with Rose and followed Dr. Aberline past those swinging doors down the hallway, to the left, into a big room with sectioned off gurneys that were mainly empty except for a man hooked up to a breathing apparatus and an older woman surrounded by doctors, her leg crooked, no doubt broken.

When he came to Holly, who'd been put into a hospital gown, she was indeed sleeping. An IV sent fluids into her arm.

After drawing the curtain around them, Bo slumped into the chair next to her, heartsick.

What if, when she woke up, she still wanted to leave?

He took her warm hand in his, placing his other palm lightly on her belly.

"Glad to see you both," he said softly. Maybe the baby could hear him, although Holly couldn't. And maybe the child could persuade her to stay, through the umbilical cord that connected them.

"You don't know how rough it was, standing out in that waiting room," Bo added. "Thinking of your mom and you in here, remembering her face on the way to the hospital because she was so afraid for you. And I was scared, too."

He rubbed Holly's tummy. It was so fascinatingly round, firm. There was a little human in there—his son or daughter.

"Thank God it's over now, and all that's left is to say how sorry I am for being such a bullheaded jerk." The words caught in his throat. "I wasn't half the dad I could've been. Or half the husband. And I was so afraid to even make an attempt to do better than that."

He brought Holly's hand to his lips, not sure he could talk anymore without losing it altogether. But the vulnerability didn't stop him from trying.

"I'm never going to go *anywhere*, not after the six months end, and not now. I'm here to stay."

Bo didn't say anything more, because he couldn't.

Besides, he knew he had gotten the point across, especially with the tears that blinded him as he leaned his head against Holly's knuckles, so grateful that she was alive and well, still carrying their child.

He only prayed that, when she woke up, she would tell him she would stay.

Holly hadn't been sleeping at all—not after Bo had sat down.

Even as exhausted and woozy as she was, it was as if she had some kind of radar that awakened her to his presence, an alarm that trilled through her every time he was near.

And that meant she'd heard Bo pouring out his soul to the baby.

Now, she held back the burning in her closed eyes, the push of heat up her chest and throat.

Bo had been able to spill his guts while she was supposedly asleep, but would he have been so forthcoming if he knew she was listening to his confessions?

Or would he have gone back to being Public Bo, where everything he said was designed to keep everyone at a distance, even though they thought they knew him?

Holly was afraid to open her eyes because she feared something even worse: that she would encounter Wounded Bo—the bruised son who thought all marriages were shams.

Maybe he was only capable of revealing his true feelings when he thought she wasn't hearing them, but his naked admissions still sent tremors through her.

He'd wanted to be a better dad, a better husband.

Did that mean he loved her though? Why couldn't he say *that?*

She risked a glance through her eyelashes. Bo was clinging to her hand, looking so distraught, looking…

Like a man in love.

Caught between not believing it and wanting to with all her heart, Holly opened her eyes all the way.

He seemed to sense it, too, and his gaze linked to hers, sending a barrage of love, trepidation, puzzlement through her.

"Holly?" he said, resting her arm down on the bed.

Her knuckles were damp from…his tears? Yes, she could see from the red of his eyes that he'd been sharply affected. A tough man, driven to despair.

It twisted her up. But his unchecked emotion began to heal her, too, although she didn't know how long that would last if Bo started dancing around their issues again.

She waited, because if he didn't make the first move, telling her what he had just told the baby, that would be it. She would know that he would never change, and she couldn't bear to live with that.

But then he started talking, his tone raw.

"I was just speaking with Hopper."

She nodded. *Talk to me. Please, Bo.*

He stroked her arm, seemingly gathering his courage.

Damn him for keeping her on this hook, damn him—

"I'm going to take better care of you from now on," he said. "I only wanted to keep all of us safe and happy."

Because he couldn't do the same for his own family back when his uncle and Steph's dad had been killed?

"But," he added, "I also tried to keep myself safe all these years, too. Too safe. And in the process, I messed things up with you and the baby."

No, you didn't, she thought, because he still had the opportunity to take what he'd started with them and run with it.

Yet it sounded as if he might be setting her up for a fall, and she braced herself.

"I have no idea how to be a good father, but I swear to you, Holly." When he looked into her eyes this time, she saw a different burning there—a determination, a soul-deep vow. "I'm going to be a real husband and father."

"And what does that mean?" Her voice sounded like a croak. "'Real'?"

"It means just what it sounds like—that I'm going to learn how to keep you guys happy forever. I'm going to give everything I've got to you, including my trust." He ran his hand up her arm. "I just hope you see fit to take me, after what we've been through."

He still hadn't said the words she really wanted to hear, and she began to close her eyes again until…

"I love you, Holly, more than I thought I could ever love anyone."

A sob racked her from the middle of her chest up, making her hitch in her breath and grab the sheet.

He got out of his seat, his gaze wide.

"I'm okay," she said. "I'm… Oh, Bo."

Bo carefully slid his arms around her, obviously mindful that she was in a hospital bed. But from the way he held her head in one hand and lovingly covered her mouth with his, it was obvious that he wished they were at home, with her happy and healthy.

As he kissed her, it was as if the sun exploded behind her eyelids, in her head, in every part of her. He made her walk on air, on rays of light, above all the failures she'd tried so hard to rise above.

Bo had helped her up just when she'd been at her lowest and now, as his lips sought hers—warm, *loved*—Holly knew that she would never sink again.

Then he ended the kiss by brushing his lips over hers.

"You forgot something at home," he said, his breath warm, intimate.

He reached into his shirt pocket, holding his grandmother's ring out to her.

As Holly's smile grew, Bo got to his knee.

"Marry me, Holly. Wear this ring for real this time?"

Her mind swirled, but she felt more grounded than ever. "Yes, Bo. Yes, yes, yes…"

She hauled in a breath as he slid the ring over her finger. It was tighter than the first time he'd put it there, but it was a much better fit.

It gleamed under the hospital lights with such clarity, like a million golden days ahead of them.

"I wish Hopper could see this," he said.

Now that he'd given her his all, she could do the same. It was safe now. It was...right.

"Hopper has a name," she said. "I asked Dr. Aberline the sex because I couldn't stand waiting to know anymore...not after tonight."

As Bo held her hand to his chest, Holly smiled, a happy tear rolling out of her eye.

"I thought we could call her Sabrina, after my mother."

He kissed Holly again, and she could imagine their child opening her own sleepy gaze, smiling in the womb, as if she couldn't wait to come out and join the family that Holly and Bo would put together, day by learning day.

And, in the future, night by moonlit night.

Bo was really in it deep, but unlike last night, when his world had almost come tumbling down around him, he was getting the hang of what to do as a husband now.

Instead of leaving notes for Holly, he served her breakfast in bed, since Dr. Aberline had deemed it safe for her patient to return home with a good dose of bed rest. And Bo was more than happy to provide for his wife.

He set the rose-patterned tray on her lap, and she smiled while perusing the wheat French toast, cantaloupe, scrambled eggs and orange juice. A wildflower in a vase accompanied the offerings; Bo hadn't been able to resist going outside to pick it for her since the sun had broken through the clouds and was already shining.

"Wow," she said. "You went all out."

He was learning how to give his all, as he'd promised, and damned if this morning wasn't half as scary as he'd anticipated after saying the grand words.

I love you.

"Back in flash," he said, returning to the kitchen to fetch his own tray.

When he returned into the room, sitting next to her on the mattress, he said, "You know that all mayors don't provide this kind of service."

"Only in Thunder Canyon," she said.

Yup, they were all moving forward: the town, Bo, Holly and Sabrina.

Together.

He took out the newspaper he'd tucked under his arm, showing her the front page while she nibbled on a piece of cantaloupe. As she scanned the contents, he watched her, loving how she did everything—from chewing the fruit to the way she read a paper.

It was going to be hell refraining from doing much besides holding her for at least the next month in bed, but it was going to be worth it.

She poked her fork at the picture that covered the front page in full color, then read the headline. "'Eureka!'"

He'd mined a fortune, all right, although the article was about how he'd been elected mayor, not about how he'd struck it rich by truly finding Holly last night.

He played with one of her curls as she smiled, still reading. When she'd finished, she grabbed his hand, holding it just over her heart. He could feel the beating of it, and the rhythm took up its place in him, too.

And they would always stay this close—no one would pull them apart. They had talked, deciding that Sabrina's parentage would be kept between them. If Alan ever came back, Bo would take him down.

Sabrina was his, just as much as Holly was.

She lowered the paper. "No mention of Charles and Di." Even the news seemed to realize that he and Holly had become their own people, that they were a world away from the ill-fated royal couple and were living a true romance.

Holly neatly folded up the paper, looking just like the woman who'd always had a plan, even if that plan only concerned how to dispose of the news each day.

But when she saw him grinning at her, she tossed that paper away, reaching up to Bo and drawing him down for a kiss.

As she lay on her side, her small juice glass shook on her tray, yet she didn't seem to care about spilling it and creating a mess. Not after what they'd been through.

Their kiss grew serious, slower, hotter, and pretty soon, Bo removed the breakfast trays to the floor, climbing back into bed.

He scooped her against him, the baby bump against his stomach, his hand in the curve above his wife's hip.

She rubbed her nose against his. "Soon, we'll have a real honeymoon."

"Being with you is honeymoon enough," he said, repeating what she'd once told a couple who'd asked him and Holly when they were going to take time to celebrate their wedding.

And Bo Clifton happily held his wife, intending never to let go, through good times and bad, for better or worse, for richer or poorer.

Together they moved forward, into their own golden days, forevermore.

* * * * *

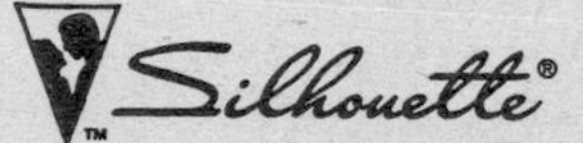

SPECIAL EDITION®

COMING NEXT MONTH

Available October 26, 2010

#2077 EXPECTING THE BOSS'S BABY
Christine Rimmer
Bravo Family Ties

#2078 ONCE UPON A PROPOSAL
Allison Leigh
The Hunt for Cinderella

#2079 THUNDER CANYON HOMECOMING
Brenda Harlen
Montana Mavericks: Thunder Canyon Cowboys

#2080 UNDER THE MISTLETOE WITH JOHN DOE
Judy Duarte
Brighton Valley Medical Center

#2081 THE BILLIONAIRE'S HANDLER
Jennifer Greene

#2082 ACCIDENTAL HEIRESS
Nancy Robards Thompson

SSECNM1010

Spotlight on

Inspirational

Wholesome romances
that touch the heart and soul.

See the next page
to enjoy a sneak peek from
the Love Inspired® Suspense
inspirational series.

CATINSPLIS10

See below for a sneak peek from our inspirational line, Love Inspired® Suspense

Enjoy this heart-stopping excerpt from RUNNING BLIND by top author Shirlee McCoy, available November 2010!

The mission trip to Mexico was supposed to be an adventure. But the thrill turns sour when Jenna Dougherty and her roommate Magdalena are kidnapped.

"It's okay. I'm here to help." The voice was as deep as the darkness, but Jenna Dougherty didn't believe the lie. She could do nothing but lie still as hands slid down her arms, felt the rope around her wrists.

"I'm going to use a knife to cut you free, Jenna. Hold still."

The cold blade of a knife pressed close to her head before her gag fell away.

"I—" she started, but her mouth was dry, and she could do nothing but suck in air.

"Shhh. Whatever needs to be said can be said when we're out of here." Nick spoke quietly, his hand gentle on her cheek. There and gone as he sliced through the ropes on her wrists and ankles.

He pulled her upright. "Come on. We may be on borrowed time."

"I can't leave my friend," Jenna rasped out.

"There's no one here. Just us."

"She has to be here." Jenna took a step away.

"There's no one here. Let's go before that changes."

"It's dark. Maybe if we find a light…"

"What did you say?"

SHLISEXP1110

"We need to turn on the light. I can't leave until I know that—"

"What can you see, Jenna?"

"Nothing."

"No shadows? No light?"

"No."

"It's broad daylight. There's light spilling in from the window I climbed in through. You can't see it?"

She went cold at his words.

"I can't see anything."

"You've got a nasty bruise on your forehead. Maybe that has something to do with it." His fingers traced the tender flesh on her forehead.

"It doesn't matter *how* it happened. I'm blind!"

Can Nick help Jenna find her friend or will chasing this trail have Jenna running blindly again into danger?

Find out in RUNNING BLIND, available in November 2010 only from Love Inspired Suspense.

SHLISEXP1110